THE SECOND URBAN FARM FRESH ROMANCE

Butterflies on Breezes

Print ISBN: 9781988068152
E-Book ISBN: 9781988068138

This is a work of fiction set in a redrawn Spokane, Washington. Businesses and locations are used fictitiously. Any resemblance to actual persons, living or dead, is coincidental.

Cover Art © 2016 Hanna Sandvig, www.bookcoverbakery.com.

Holy Bible, New Living Translation, copyright © 1996, 2004, 2015 by Tyndale House Foundation. Used by permission of Tyndale House Publishers Inc., Carol Stream, Illinois 60188. All rights reserved.

First edition, GreenWords Media, 2016

THE SECOND URBAN FARM FRESH ROMANCE

Butterflies on Breezes

VALERIE COMER

GreenWords Media

Dedication

For Lynn

Acknowledgments

This has been a fun story to write! If you're familiar with Spokane, Washington, you may (sort of) recognize the Bridgeview neighborhood... with adaptations. I definitely took some liberties for the sake of the story on several counts, which I hope you'll forgive. Manito Park is real, however, along with its beautiful Nishinomiya Japanese Garden, Rose Hill, and the lovely butterfly garden adjacent to Joel E. Ferris Perennial Garden.

Thanks to Robin, Rebecca, Donna, Elizabeth, Anna, and Debbie for having a great eye for detail as beta readers, and also to my entire street team for cheering me on throughout the process and helping fine-tune the story description. You ladies are so appreciated every day!

As ever, hugs and thanks to Nicole, without whom I wouldn't have half the success I do today. You rock as both a friend and an editor.

I'm always thankful for my fellow inspirational romance author friends at Inspy Romance and my Christian Indie Authors group. Thanks to you all for walking the journey with me both personally and professionally.

Thanks to Leah and Josh for modeling for the cover and to Hanna of Book Cover Bakery for pulling together yet another delightful romance cover.

Thanks to the many readers who've emailed, sharing their excitement to shift from their beloved Farm Fresh Romance series to the new urbanized version. I couldn't do it without all of you — or at least I wouldn't want to.

Thanks to my husband, Jim, for research trips to Spokane and talking through scenarios — to say nothing of constant love and support — and to my kids and grandgirls for cheering me on and embracing the idiosyncrasies of having an author for a mom and grandmother.

Thanks to Jesus, without whom I would not have stories to tell. If there is any breeze lifting my wings, let me point to Him, the source of all light and life.

Books by Valerie Comer

Farm Fresh Romance Novels

Raspberries and Vinegar
Wild Mint Tea
Sweetened with Honey
Dandelions for Dinner
Plum Upside Down
Berry on Top

Riverbend Romance Novellas

Secretly Yours
Pinky Promise
Sweet Serenade
Team Bride
Merry Kisses

Urban Farm Fresh Romance Novels

Secrets of Sunbeams
Butterflies on Breezes
Memories of Mist

Christmas in Montana Romance Series

More Than a Tiara
Other Than a Halo

Chapter 1

M Y GRANDDAUGHTER SEEMS to think you're the right person for this job."

Linnea Ranta quailed under the elderly woman's skeptical look. "I've worked for my dad's landscaping business since I was in high school. I'm sure I can make your dreams a reality." At least, if Marietta Santoro could put those ideas into words or even sketches. So far it had been mostly hand-waving.

"Humph." The Italian grandmother pointed to the weed-filled lot beyond the wire-mesh fence. Every inch of this side was packed with flowers and vegetables with every tidy row pointing due north. It was no wonder Marietta couldn't stand the sight of the disaster next door. "I want a fence around that. I want raised beds for the neighbors to grow vegetables. I want a watering system and a bench over in that corner under the sycamore."

Maybe Linnea didn't want the job after all. She wasn't a carpenter, and it didn't sound like Marietta had any vision for aesthetics. But it wasn't like she could turn down the first job that hadn't been assigned by Dad. This was her chance to prove she was more than hired help.

She ducked as a hummingbird zinged to an overhead feeder. Wings flashed as another one chased it away. "I see you like birds."

"*Si*. Who does not?"

"If you're keeping the sycamore — which I'm definitely a fan of — we could create a bit of a bird habitat in that area. Add some seed-bearing plants and maybe a birdbath." Linnea snuck a glance at the older woman.

Marietta nodded thoughtfully as she stared through the fence. "That is a possibility. The little ones would like to watch birds."

Maybe this could work after all. "I like your ideas, Marietta. Do you want me to find a builder for the structural needs, or do you have someone in mind?"

The old woman smiled. "Did I not tell you already? That boy who plays the piano at church when Francesca can't. He will do it."

Linnea froze. Logan Dermott? Every time his hands touched the keyboard, the world faded away, and Linnea was transported to heavenly realms. He felt the music. He lived the music. In some ways, he *was* the music.

And she'd never missed a Sunday in the six weeks he'd been attending Bridgeview Bible Church, just in case he was playing.

"You'll be in charge, if you take this on. It will be up to you to tell him where to put all those raised beds. There's a slope..." Marietta scrunched her face thoughtfully. "Well, you figure it out. When you come up with a cost list, please show it to Raimondo, and he will give approval or offer suggestions."

In charge? Tell Logan what to do? Linnea gulped. Answering to Marietta's son Ray was nothing compared to spending time with Logan Dermott for weeks to come. She tried to imagine giving him orders. Her hands turned clammy. Maybe she should turn Marietta down. Tell her she was too busy. She'd been asked to volunteer, and this was a mighty big job. But getting the chance to actually design a garden from scratch would be well worth it if Marietta would give her a good recommendation at the other end.

"Sounds good."

Had that been her voice? Linnea's innards trembled. No, she should have declined, not agreed. Still, Logan Dermott? But what if he already had a girlfriend? Oh, there was no one in Spokane or surely she'd have come to church with him, but maybe somewhere else. A guy like him, so good-looking, confident, and talented, must have women hanging onto him wherever he went.

"He should be here at any time." Marietta checked her watch, clucking impatiently. "He is late."

Linnea took a deep shuddering breath. There wouldn't be time to brace herself for this meeting unless she hurried away right now. But what would that gain? Nothing. She'd agreed to work with him, and it would only prolong her suffering if she put off their first meeting. She wiped her hands down her denim pants.

Cheerful whistling came from behind her.

She whirled to see Logan Dermott rounding the corner of Marietta's white stucco home, wearing faded jeans threadbare in one knee. A white T-shirt, looking a little the worse for wear, stretched over his muscular torso. Tousled hair skimmed his shoulders, and he hadn't shaved for several days by the look of his scruff.

Linnea swallowed hard. He looked amazing in dark wash jeans and a button-down shirt for church, but a real man who worked for a living was so much more attractive.

"Logan Dermott. You are late." Marietta sounded reproachful.

He grinned at her, a dimple flashing in his right cheek. "I beg your pardon." He took the old woman's hand and kissed it as he bowed over it. Then his gaze rested on Linnea. "I have not had the pleasure of meeting this lovely lady. Where have you been hiding her, Marietta? Is she another of your granddaughters?"

Oh, he was good.

"Not my granddaughter, no." Marietta patted his face. "This is Linnea Ranta from over on Riverside Avenue. She works with her father in his landscaping business. She is going to oversee the community garden project next door. Linnea, this is Logan. He is new to Bridgeview."

His smile widened as he slowly looked Linnea over and finally met her gaze again. "It is my pleasure to meet you, but to work with you on this garden?" He clasped her hand in both of his. "I am looking forward to every moment."

"I, um, it's nice to meet you, too." Somehow she got the words past her lips. His hands were warm and callused. Both his thumbs caressed hers. He was way over the top in his intensity, but somehow it didn't seem too much. Not when warmth that had nothing to do with the July sunshine radiated through her body.

She tugged her hand free. A cloud came over the sun, though there wasn't a single one in the brilliant blue sky, reflected in his twinkling eyes.

"Linnea is as talented as she is *bella*," Marietta said, resting her hand on Logan's arm. "I think I have made a good choice with the two of you."

The smug smile on the old woman's face did nothing to reassure Linnea. Was she really wanting a garden created, or was she playing matchmaker? Because a self-assured man like Logan wouldn't take something like that sitting down. He'd make his own choices, and it wouldn't likely be someone like Linnea. She'd been a shadowed hosta all her life and, though she longed for the light, he'd be looking for a showy flower that danced in the sunshine.

What was Marietta up to? The neighborhood matriarch looked like she'd swallowed the proverbial canary. So she was setting them up for more than a garden. Did she do this kind of thing often? Well, there was no harm in playing along for now. Linnea looked a little shy, but she was certainly pretty. Plus, he'd already agreed to help with the garden. It didn't much matter with whom he worked. A bit of flirting wouldn't go amiss, so long as he kept it in check.

Logan turned to Marietta. "How do you expect me to get any work done with such a beautiful woman nearby? I'm sure I'll be too distracted."

"There is no rush. It is too late to grow most things yet this summer. We only need to be ready for springtime."

He didn't miss the sharp look Linnea gave Marietta. So he wasn't the only one noticing.

"Would you like to walk around the space with us?" Logan gestured to the gate leading through the wire-mesh fence to the unkempt lot next door. "Perhaps give some ideas as to what you'd like to see where?"

Marietta set her hand over her heart. "No, I am tired. You two go ahead. When you've had a chance to draw some preliminary plans, bring them to my son Raimondo. If he approves, you may present him with a list of materials to purchase."

Logan had met Ray Santoro several times around the neighborhood and at church. The man would definitely be easier to deal with than his eccentric mother. "Sounds good." He turned to Linnea. "Do you have a few minutes now, or shall we set another time to do a walk about?"

Linnea's gaze flicked to his then away. "We could take a few minutes now if you have time."

"Always time for a beautiful woman." He took Linnea's arm and nodded at Marietta. "We'll get back to you later."

Marietta touched her thumb and forefinger together as she smiled. "I will wait in eagerness."

Logan steered Linnea toward the gate and ushered her into the other yard. "Marietta is something else, isn't she," he murmured, angling his head close to hers. "She wants more than a garden."

Linnea's long blond hair brushed against his arm like a rippling breeze as she turned to face him. "I don't have to do this. She can find someone else."

She wasn't his usual type being so thin. Her white tank top showed off minimal assets, and now he knew where the term skinny jeans had come from. But her face was definitely attractive, and her blue eyes seemed shadowed with something deeper.

"Or we can play along for now. I am definitely in need of something to do, and working with you to transform this space sounds like a terrific way to spend time." Logan grinned. "Who knows? Maybe her fond wishes will come true."

Was that a pink flush shooting across her face? Interesting. He'd have to be careful. Hurting someone was never part of the package.

Linnea pulled away from his touch and strode to the middle of the lot. "She wants sixteen four-by-twelve-foot raised beds, so those will take up almost half of the area. We'll need to do some terracing, though."

He wandered closer, careful to leave some distance between them. "It's not much of a slope. I'm sure we can manage that."

"We'll need paths between them wide enough for a wheelbarrow." She spread her hands apart. "So, a good three feet. Maybe four."

Logan nodded. "Makes sense."

"I'm not sure what she's told you. I know she wants you to construct a picket fence around to keep the neighborhood dogs out."

"And the raised beds themselves, as well as some benches and a gazebo."

"A gazebo? She didn't mention that to me."

"I think she wants to keep me busy for a while." He grinned wryly.

Linnea shot him an unreadable glance.

"But I'm in it for whatever you need. I can help with the terracing. Digging. Laying sod. Whatever you need." Transforming ninety-thousand square feet would take a lot of digging. A lot of time. He could think of worse ways to spend it, especially since his housemate was dating the girl next door and seemed to never be home.

"I can bring in Dad's Bobcat to do the heavy lifting."

His eyebrows rose. "You can drive a Bobcat?"

"And why not?" Her fists landed on her narrow hips. "I've been working with my dad since I was in high school. This isn't the first time I've encountered real work."

Logan could see definition in those biceps, small as they were. "Okay, I believe you." He raised both hands. "You're the boss. I'm just the serf, here to do your bidding. Whatever you want done, I am at your command."

Her face reddened again. It was going to be far too easy to fluster this woman, but walking on eggshells belied his very personality.

Chapter 2

"HOW DID IT GO?" Mom asked. "Are you taking on Marietta's job?"

Linnea leaned against the counter. "Yes, I think I am."

"How much is she paying you?"

Ah, the million-dollar question. Like Mom was going to understand. "I'm getting good experience, masterminding an entire community garden with raised beds and a bird and butterfly garden."

Her mother paused with the fridge open. "What are you not telling me?"

Uh… everything? Man, Linnea needed to move out of the house. She might be twenty-four, but her parents still treated her like a teenager. If only Dad paid her enough to rent a place on her own, like in that small apartment building over in Bridgeview. She'd seen a vacancy sign on the red brick building when she drove by on her way home from Marietta's.

"You're volunteering, aren't you? That woman is so cheap. I can't believe she would ask you to do it for free.

Your time is valuable, Linnea. You can't waste it on an old woman's whims. You don't even know her that well."

Linnea closed her eyes. Was Mom done already?

"Linnea. Be strong. Take charge."

How could she take charge when her parents persisted in telling her what to do? Maybe she should look for another job. Could there be another landscaping or lawn care business in Spokane that would hire her and pay her what she was worth? But then she'd have to give Dad as a reference, and he'd end her dreams right there. Although Marietta could give a reference if Linnea did a good job on the community garden.

"Linnea Marie. Cat got your tongue?"

"It's all volunteer, Mom. I have my own reasons for taking this on. Don't worry about it."

Her mother closed the fridge door and stared at her. "Your father won't be impressed. He saves his pro bono work for real charities."

"I'm doing this in my free time. It doesn't affect you or Dad in any way." She remembered her voice saying she could borrow Dad's Bobcat. Well, he didn't need it on Saturdays, and she'd pay for the fuel it took. Or she'd bill Marietta for that. Whatever.

"Your father will be home soon for supper. We'll see what he has to say."

"Mom, are you seriously telling me that my life isn't my own after work hours? That I can't have any hobbies or make friends without your approval?"

Her mother tsked. "Of course not. But still."

"Then leave it, okay?" Linnea walked over to the sink and poured herself a glass of water, her hands shaking. It was time. Past time. "I won't be home for supper, Mom. No need to wait for me."

That got Mom's attention. "But you must eat. Look at you. Thin as a rail. How will you ever catch a man, so skinny?" Her hands carved an hour-glass in the air. "Men like a bit of flesh to squeeze."

Maybe not as much as Mom had. And who wanted her body squeezed, anyway? Linnea managed a smile. "I'm naturally thin. I'm fine. Healthy. I'll see you later." It hadn't seemed to turn off Logan Dermott. Wow, that man could schmooze. She'd try not to take him seriously. She'd seen him in action after church, tossing flirty remarks at various single women. Not at Hailey North, though. Hailey might be a successful business owner, but she didn't have a clue about men and didn't seem to notice Logan was completely uninterested. Not that Linnea was an expert, but even she could see that much.

She sure wasn't telling her parents all the complex reasons she had for accepting. Getting to know Logan was a bonus. Or not.

If she thought her mom had reacted badly, it was nothing to the gasket Dad would blow.

Linnea grabbed her keys and strode out to her truck. There was only one place she could think of to soothe her frayed nerves. A few minutes later she pulled into Manito Park. The rose gardens had been about to bloom the last time she'd taken time to walk through them.

Today the heady fragrance permeated the air. Linnea breathed deeply, filling her lungs with the sweet scent from the thousands — maybe millions — of riotous blossoms in every color and every variety that could possibly grow in the Inland Northwest. She walked reverently down the grassy center toward the sundial and pergolas at the far end. A fat gray squirrel darted between the bushes and disappeared amid the conifers beyond.

Why couldn't she get over her irrational need to please her father? Her brother Dan didn't have that need. He was working as a used-car salesman and living with a woman with two kids, neither of them his. Contrast that to Dad's pride in the eldest, David Junior, who was a rising attorney and could do no wrong. At least in Dad's eyes.

She just wanted to be herself. She loved landscaping. She'd love to help people's dreams of a backyard oasis become a reality. Instead, she mowed lawns and trimmed hedges while Dad did the few requested designs. Taking care of yards was okay, but she didn't like using all the pesticides and herbicides he believed in. For him, everything had to be flawless and green. The emerald color, not the environmental practice.

The rose garden reminded her too much of Dad with its symmetrical beds, yet it was downright free-form compared to the formal sunken garden beyond the conservatory.

Linnea strode back the way she'd come, trailing her hand on the native rock wall that lined the curving descent to the parking lot. She'd needed to smell the roses, but her favorite spot was on the other side of the parking lot.

The butterfly garden, a concrete bird bath in the center, lay nestled in a rounded boxwood hedge. Stone paths curved amid the herbs and flowers. A few Painted Lady butterflies fluttered from plant to plant.

Linnea settled onto one of the wooden benches, her spirit easing immediately.

"Lord?" she whispered. "Please show me what to do about Dad and Mom. I'm not sure how much more of this I can take, but it's so hard to break free of all I've ever known."

The vision of a butterfly struggling to escape its chrysalis focused in her mind.

She grinned wryly. "Is that some sort of message, Lord? Nature takes over for caterpillars. It's not like they have a choice whether to fight their way out or not." She, on the other hand, had a choice, and it was definitely time to begin the process.

Logan slid onto the bench by his electronic keyboard. His housemate, Jacob Riehl, was out somewhere with his girlfriend, so Logan didn't feel the need to plug in the headset. Not that Jacob usually minded him playing, though Logan preferred music much louder than his friend.

His fingers rippled over the keys, seeking a song that suited his mood. What did he want to express to his Maker? Nothing seemed quite right. After doodling through half a dozen, he wandered into the kitchen and grabbed a package of cookies from the farmers' market. He slid the patio door open and settled onto an Adirondack chair while he pulled out the first cookie.

This wasn't like him. When had he last been pensive or restless? Never mind about the restless. That had sent him overseas several times, backpacking in the Andes, boating down the Nile, scuba diving off the Papua New Guinea coast. Since he'd left home, he'd only worked long enough to fund his next adventure.

It's time to put down roots.

Really?

Logan sat upright in the curved chair. Whoa. Where had that thought come from? He'd moved to Spokane with his buddy with the full expectation of wandering on in a year at most. There were many places he wanted to see yet. Patagonia. Iceland. The great wall of China.

Did he really want adventure more than a little house like the one behind him? Than he wanted a wife? Children?

But this was ridiculous. After his messed-up childhood, he'd never wanted to get married. He'd been shuffled from one parent to the other without notice, as had his sisters, although each had different fathers, of course.

He could be faithful to one woman. He could be a different dad than his had been. History didn't have to repeat itself.

Linnea slid into his mind. She seemed to have some issues but, hey, didn't everyone? They were going to be seeing a lot of each other over the next few months. He wouldn't be able to avoid her wistful blue eyes, but he could avoid getting too involved before he headed overseas. Leaving a broken heart behind was never part of the plan.

Although that was laughable. Who was he to break hearts?

He remembered Linnea's furtive glances and her blushing cheeks, but that was just because she didn't really know him. They'd part as friends when he'd saved up enough. Maybe he'd go to India this time.

Somehow travel seemed a little less alluring than it had before.

Linnea stood at the salad counter at Main Market Co-op, mindful of the fact that heavier items, like boiled eggs, would add to the cost of her build-your-own salad. But she'd skipped dinner at home, and she needed some protein as well as greens.

"Linnea! What a coincidence. I was thinking of tracking you down."

She glanced up to see her friend Jasmine Santoro. "Hey! How are you doing?"

"I'm doing well. I'm moving my massage clinic over to West Main."

"Oh, that's great." Linnea could use a massage or two herself. "Congratulations."

"Thanks. Papa helped fund it so I'd move back to Bridgeview." Jasmine rolled her eyes. "You know what parents are like. They just can't seem to let go."

Oh, Linnea knew all right. If she had a job in North Spokane, though, no amount of funding from her father would rein her back in. She managed a chuckle. "Too true."

"I've had a look inside one of those apartments in Bridgeview Manor. What a cool building! So much history and character, but all they have available is a two-bedroom unit right now. Where are you living?"

Linnea's heart jumped. Could this be the answer? "With my parents, but I've been thinking of getting my own place. Are you looking for a roommate?"

"I am, if it's the right person." Jasmine grinned. "Pretty sure I could trust you not to have loud parties until two in the morning. Want to go halfers with me?" She quoted the rental price. "Is that too much? Papa said he'd put down the damage deposit if I decided to go for it. He'll hold out his hand for the refund when I move out, so no need to worry about chipping in for that part."

"You know, I'm really interested. Is there a chance I could see the unit before I commit?" To say nothing of thinking how she'd broach this to Dad. Jasmine's was so much nicer. Everyone in the neighborhood knew and respected Raimondo Santoro.

"I don't see why not. Let me call the manager and set up a time. What's your schedule like?"

"I'm free any evening, at least if I know in advance. Your grandmother has enlisted me to oversee the building of a community garden in that empty lot. I hear I have you to thank for the recommendation, by the way."

"You're welcome." Jasmine grinned. "You and Logan Dermott, right?"

Heat flushed across her cheeks. Grr. Why did everything show on her face? "He'll be doing the construction parts."

"Nonna is up to something, you know."

Nothing Linnea hadn't suspected with the conniving look on Marietta's face. She shrugged.

"Mostly she is trying to keep Logan away from me. She has it in her head that I must marry a Bridgeview boy, and of course Logan doesn't qualify, being a newcomer. If I don't marry a local man, he'd better be Italian." Jasmine shook her head. "Like Nonna can order love."

It wasn't so much Marietta trying to set Linnea up with Logan as to protect her granddaughter from the man. So much for any courage the project had given her.

"Hey, did I say something wrong? I'm not interested in Logan. He can play that piano like an angel, but he's not the man for me. Nonna needn't have worried, but no one can tell her anything she doesn't want to hear."

He was a bit rogue for Linnea, too. That alone should be enough to douse her feelings with ice water, but somehow it didn't. There was just something about his confidence that attracted her to him.

"I think we'll do well in an apartment together. I was hoping you'd say yes."

Jasmine had sought her out for this purpose? That was an honor. The Italian girl might also be introverted, but she seemed much more secure.

Linnea's heart warmed. "It would be for the end of July, right?" That would give her some time to ease into the conversation with her parents.

"It's empty right now, and the manager offered to pro-rate July's rent. We could move in as early as next weekend."

Whoa. Was she really ready to do this? Dad wouldn't fire her, would he? No. He'd hassle her, but he wouldn't go that far. Linnea nodded slowly. "Give the manager a call."

Chapter 3

"OGAN. IT IS *BENE* to see you." Marietta peered past him before focusing on his face. "Nothing has happened next door yet that I can see."

It had been all of three days. "There's been lots going on behind the scenes. I've been working on material lists." He held out an empty canning jar. "Thanks so much for the pasta sauce. My housemate and I really enjoyed it the other night."

"You're welcome." Marietta accepted the jar. "And Linnea? What has she been doing?"

"That's the real reason I stopped by. I discovered I don't have her phone number, and was hoping you could give it to me. That way I can find out where she is with the project."

"The project." The old woman's eyes gleamed.

"Yep." Logan kept his voice easy. He wouldn't let this busybody, of any person in Bridgeview, know he'd spent more than a little time in the past few days recalling Linnea's slender frame, flushing face, and pretty blue eyes.

"I'll get that for you. Come inside."

Logan followed her into a kitchen that smelled of garlic and tomatoes. He'd seen a greenhouse in her backyard, hadn't he? Otherwise where would she be getting this many ripe tomatoes from in mid-July?

Marietta tipped the jar upside-down in the dishwasher.

Apparently it wasn't clean enough to join the row of gleaming quarts marching down the granite countertop in the huge kitchen. If she were starting over canning new sauces now, no wonder she'd been willing to part with an older jar.

"Aha. Here it is." Marietta pulled a slip of paper from a desk drawer. "Let me find something to write her number on."

"No need." Logan crossed the space. "I'll just enter it into my phone."

"That newfangled technology," mumbled Marietta, as he added a new contact to his list and tapped in Linnea's information.

Indeed, an old-fashioned phone with a cord curling all the way to the floor hung on the wall beside the desk. He'd wager a bet she could talk on that thing from anywhere in the kitchen and possibly half the remainder of the house. She probably did so for hours at a time.

Logan clicked his phone off. "Thanks. That's all I needed today."

"She is a *bene* girl. *Bella.*"

He forced a smile. "She seems very nice, yes." He turned to go when the back door opened, and a guy about his own age sauntered in.

"Nonna. You are looking well." The newcomer kissed Marietta's cheek.

"Pietro. Thank you." She patted his face. "Have you met Logan Dermott? He and his friend are renting my house down on Water Street."

The guy stuck out his hand. "Pleased to meet you. Nonna insists on Pietro, but everyone else calls me Peter." He held his hand beside his mouth to direct the next words to Logan. "In fact, it's Peter on my birth certificate. Don't tell her."

Marietta swatted her grandson's arm. "Don't talk nonsense."

Logan bit back a grin. He'd even take a grandmother like Marietta just to get a real sense of family. Dad's mom was so busy with her San Francisco real estate career she had no time for anyone, while his maternal grandmother had no ambition whatsoever. Like mother, like daughter. In either case, he didn't have family like this. He should do more for his younger sisters.

"I came for some cookies, Nonna." Peter winked at Logan. "I need the sustenance before I head over to shoot hoops. You wouldn't want me to die of starvation, would you?"

"You're an impossible boy." But Marietta reached for the cookie jar that looked like a fat chef with a mustache.

Peter dug in for a handful and pointed his chin at Logan. "Have you had my nonna's baking yet? You need to try these."

Marietta offered the container to him, and Logan took two. "Thanks."

"Hey, do you play basketball? We could use another guy on the court."

He didn't need to think twice. Jacob was so quiet he was barely company at the best of times and, with Eden in the picture, he was even less entertaining. Logan needed new friends. *More* friends. "I play a bit." That was mostly honest. "I'd love to check it out."

Peter jerked his head toward the door. "Come on then."

Half an hour later, Logan knew for a fact he was in way over his head. This three-on-three was no casual pickup game. These guys were rad. Logan felt like a kindergartener in their midst. He'd managed to block a couple of baskets, but that had been sheer luck.

He was going to die, and it had been a long time since he'd felt more alive. Sweat poured off his entire body, and his chest heaved. He struggled for air as he braced both hands on his knees. When he could gasp out words, he asked, "You guys play for the NBA or what?"

Peter smacked Logan on the back, nearly toppling him. "No, but we finished Hoopfest in the top five percent."

"Hoopfest?" That sounded vaguely familiar.

"Seven thousand teams converged on Spokane in late June for some three-on-three. This was one of the courts." Peter eyed him. "How could you have missed it?"

"Uh. I only moved here in June. I do remember seeing games going on, but I was busy settling in."

"Okay, you're forgiven. For this year, anyway. Where'd you come from?"

"I was raised near Tacoma." Not that he'd been there in years. For that matter, he'd lived a lot of places since, and none of *them* seemed like home, either. Was he seriously starting to crave a deeper connection?

In his thoughts, Linnea smiled at him shyly, her cheeks rosy. Yeah... no. He'd steer away from someone who'd be that easy to hurt.

Linnea hauled another box up the concrete steps from the curb and through the propped-open door. Up a thousand stairs. Okay, only two flights and down the hall, but still. This was going to take all evening. Good thing Jasmine had some furniture, having rented a house with several friends for the past five years. Linnea had nothing to bring but her own clothes, books, and personal items. She didn't even have a bedroom set. Dad had blown a gasket at the very thought of her removing her childhood furniture, so Jasmine had scrounged up a loaner bed and dresser from her parents' basement.

Don't look back. Don't look back.

Not that looking back would do any good. Even if she repented in dust and ashes and crawled back to Dad, he'd hold this against her for the next decade. No, there was no returning.

As long as he didn't fire her.

Linnea gritted her teeth. By the look on his face, he'd thought about it. She'd half expected him to demand the keys to the company truck she drove, but he hadn't. Not yet, anyway.

She deposited the box on the growing pile in her new room and paused at the pair of large double-hung windows. This view of the Spokane River wouldn't get old anytime soon. She could make out the roof of the house Logan and Jacob rented from Marietta down a couple of streets, and the new, fancy development of Kendall Yards on the high banks on the north shore.

Inside, scuffed wooden floors and creamy, old-fashioned stucco walls provided a welcome change from the dated, faded carpet and wallpaper in her old room. She took a deep breath. She could do this. After all, she'd already done it. Let the chips fall where they may.

"Hey, need a hand to haul more stuff up here? I saw more boxes in your truck."

She turned to take in Jasmine's brother Alex leaning against the door frame, hands in his jeans pockets. Of medium height with curly dark hair and an easy grin like most of the Santoro men, he'd been a casual friend since high school.

"I wouldn't say no, but Jasmine probably needs more help."

Alex shook his head. "She went to get a couple of pizzas from the bakery." He rubbed his belly. "She knows how to treat her help right."

Heat crept up Linnea's cheeks.

"Hey, no worries. I didn't mean that you didn't. It was Jas's call. She's excited to be rooming with you."

It would be nice if not every single thought she had spread across her face. "Thanks," she managed to get out.

"Look, I'll give you a hand with the rest of your boxes, okay? I need something to do while I wait, or Jas will think I don't deserve any pizza."

"We can't let a growing boy starve to death." Linnea brushed past him and through the barren living room.

Alex fell into step beside her in the corridor and nudged her with his elbow. "And here I thought we were beyond that stage. I haven't been a growing boy for a few years now. You hadn't noticed?"

She glanced up to see his aggrieved expression, tempered by the twinkle in his eyes. Seriously. No one had shown any interest in her in eons. Now two men were flirting with her? Not that she'd seen Logan for a few days.

Her cell phone rang as she jogged down the last flight. Unknown number. She hesitated on the landing outside the

33

building. Did she dare answer? It wasn't Dad, though. His name would come up.

She thumbed it on and leaned on the railing. "Hello?"

"Hi, Linnea? It's Logan. I got your number off Marietta. I hope you don't mind."

Below on the street, Alex loaded two smaller boxes into his arms and came back toward her.

"Um, no. That's fine. We should have thought to exchange numbers the other day."

Alex raised his eyebrows at her words and walked past her.

"I was just checking to see if you'd made any progress on laying out the specs. I've begun gathering a materials list, but I want to run it past you."

Guilt flooded her. "I haven't done a thing on the project. I'm sorry."

"Hey, no worries. We're volunteers, so she can't hold us to a timeline."

Linnea let out a breath. "Thanks for understanding. An opportunity came up suddenly for me to move, and that's occupied my attention for the past few days."

"I bet. That's great, though. Where are you moving? Hopefully not too far from Bridgeview." His voice teased at her.

"No, into the only apartment building in the neigh-borhood. Jasmine Santoro found the suite, and we're going to share it."

"You wouldn't happen to be standing outside leaning on a wrought-iron railing, would you?"

He could see her? Linnea straightened and scanned the area. Where was he?

A guy waved from the basketball court under the bridge half a block away. He definitely had the shoulder-length messy hair Logan sported, not so typical in Bridgeview. The man strolled toward her, his hand by his ear.

"Ah, it *is* you. We looked at that building and called the management. They didn't have any openings for June first, so we wound up with Marietta's house. It's worked out pretty well for Jacob and me."

"Th-that's great." She stared at him as he closed the distance. When he started up the steps, she realized she could turn her phone off. She'd record his incoming number as a contact later. "Hey."

Logan grinned and leaned on the rail beside her. He smelled like a guy who'd been working hard, not at all unpleasant.

"Excuse me. Peter and company just indoctrinated me in three-on-three. I had no idea what I was doing next to them."

She smiled. "Yes, this neighborhood usually enters a few teams into Hoopfest. Peter's team did very well the past few years."

Logan shook his head. "It's good exercise, I'll grant you that much. It will take me a few days to prepare to do it again, though."

"Only a few days?" She glanced at him, curious. Footsteps clattered down the staircase behind her. She turned to see Alex wearing an inscrutable expression. "I'm sorry, Logan. Now's not a good time to chat. Not when Alex is giving me a hand unloading my truck."

"Oh, hey, let me help." Logan pointed at the half-empty pickup below. "All that goes up? Just show me where."

"The name's Alex Santoro." Jasmine's brother's eyebrows rose as he stared Logan down, hand outstretched.

"Logan Dermott. Pleased to meet you."

The handshake went on a little longer than normal. What was going on here? This couldn't be happening. They were both just trying to make her feel better by making her feel desirable. It didn't mean anything, even though they stared at each other like two bulldogs.

"Excuse me." Linnea edged behind Alex and ran down the steps. She grabbed a box only to find both men behind her, reaching for another. Whew. The moment had passed.

Chapter 4

*H*E'D THOUGHT THE basketball game had taken everything out of him, but he'd been wrong. Logan dredged deep for enough energy to haul more boxes — bigger, heavier boxes — up the two flights of stairs than Alex Santoro.

Which was ridiculous. If Linnea had a boyfriend, what was that to him? Nothing. He'd never asked her any questions where *Alex* could have been the answer. Like, 'are you dating someone?' 'Yes, my amazing and hunky boyfriend, Alex, who could eat you for breakfast.'

Telling himself this every trip up and down the stairs did nothing to curtail him. The same seemed true of Alex, who bounded down the stairs empty-handed every time Logan staggered up with the biggest load he could carry. That was a good sign, right? Alex wouldn't have tried to break the bones in Logan's hand if he were secure in Linnea's love.

But who said Logan wanted it? Was he merely reacting to the other guy's bravado?

A motorbike swerved to a stop behind the pickup. The rider removed her helmet and shook long dark hair loose. "Hey, Logan."

Logan nearly tripped over the curb. Jasmine rode a Harley-Davidson? He shook his head, but it was still her.

She swung her leg over and unstrapped two pizza boxes. "Wow, you've got Linnea's truck nearly unloaded. I hope you're staying for dinner. It just arrived."

"Too bad Dermott has to be somewhere else." Alex stood above him on the landing. "What kind did you get, sis?"

That explained a lot. Maybe. Logan grinned. *Game on.* "I think you misunderstood, Alex. Dinner sounds great. I left the smallest box for you. Hope you can handle it." He mounted the steps and swept past the other guy.

Childish? Sure, but it was kind of fun to watch Alex's jaw drop before closing and clamping. To hear Jasmine's snicker.

Upstairs, Logan deposited his burden. "Jasmine's right behind me with pizza."

Linnea turned from where she hung clothes in her new closet. "Sounds good. I'm starved." She hooked a hanger holding a pink dress over the rail.

That would look amazing on her, actually. He hadn't seen her in anything but jeans and tanks. Did she go to church at Bridgeview Bible? He wracked his brain, but came up blank. He needed to know a bit more about her before he conceded to Alex Santoro and walked away.

He held out his hand. "Come on, then. The rest can wait."

She didn't take his hand, but he hadn't expected her to. Still, resting it on the small of her back to direct her to the small round table was a natural next movement. He didn't miss Alex's glare, but it was easy to ignore as he pulled out a chair for Linnea and seated her.

"Can I give you a hand with anything?" He turned to Jasmine.

"Sure, want to dig some glasses out of that box on the counter?" She jutted her chin. "Alex, I already set the plates in the cupboard beside the sink. Grab four?"

Alex elbowed past Logan. "I know what you're doing," he growled in a low voice. "Don't mess with her."

Logan smirked. "Her choice, isn't it?" He unwrapped glasses from between cloth napkins and carried them to the table. Second thought, he grabbed the napkins, too.

Jasmine pulled a tall jar of iced tea from the nearly empty fridge before sitting across from Linnea.

At least Logan wouldn't have to jockey Alex for position. On the other hand, nothing would protect him from the other guy's direct glare through the meal.

"Would you ask the blessing, Alex?"

He shot his sister an unreadable glance. "Sure." His prayer was short, sweet, and to the point.

Jasmine tipped open the first pizza box, releasing the full aromatic force.

Logan reached for the first piece and slid it onto Linnea's plate. If Jasmine hadn't been quick enough to get her own, he'd have served her, too. As it was, he put the next slice on his own plate. "Thanks, Jasmine. This smells amazing. I appreciate the invitation to join you."

Jasmine grinned. "It looks like you've earned it. Thanks for helping."

"He only got here twenty minutes ago."

Nice one, Alex. Logan smiled at the other man. "So true. I'd have been here earlier if I'd known I was needed. As it is, I ran into your cousin Peter and he invited me to play some three-on-three. Said they were short a guy."

Alex's gaze hardened. "I told him I was giving Jas and Linnea a hand today. We could've practiced tomorrow."

"Oh, sorry to take your place." *Take that any way you want, Santoro.* "I don't mind admitting I haven't played much basketball before. They whupped me, but I'm still alive."

Jasmine's eyes danced. Linnea darted quick glances between him and Alex. Apparently they were fooling no one. That might make it easier when the time came to put Alex firmly in his place.

No way. How could he be having these thoughts? He barely knew Linnea. He wasn't going to settle down for years and years, not until he'd seen the remaining reaches of the planet. Casual dating was fine, but that was for a certain type of woman. Someone who understood it was just for innocent short-term fun.

Linnea didn't seem like that sort of woman.

So it was simple, really. They'd do the garden project together and part as friends. The last thing he wanted was to see Linnea hurt. Not by him. But not by Alex Santoro, either.

Linnea squirmed in her chair, barely able to summon the courage to reach for a second piece of pizza. She didn't need one, anyway, not with the way her gut churned thanks to Alex's and Logan's posturing. Neither of them really cared about her, so why would they act like this? She'd known Alex since high school, and he'd never given her a second glance, even when the youth group hung out at the bustling Santoro house. If he harbored deep affection, he'd certainly had plenty of time to reveal it before tonight.

But Logan. He made her heart speed up, even though she barely knew him. He oozed that kind of charm without even trying. Half the single women at church vied for his attention, which he cheerfully divided between them. The other half figured Hailey North would nail him down after all and that would be that.

See, they'd be a good match, much as it pained Linnea to think it. Two confident, flirty extroverts, giving as good as they received.

Linnea liked Hailey fine. Hailey had been a senior and busy with her own friends when Linnea's family had moved to Spokane, so they didn't know each other all that well. Hailey and her cousin owned a bakery, and Linnea mowed lawns. Their paths rarely crossed.

Jasmine's voice broke through her reverie. "Have more pizza, Linnea?"

"No, I'm good. Thanks."

Jasmine tipped the box toward her. "You've worked harder than that."

Logan slid a slice to her plate and smiled right into her eyes. "She's right."

Everyone was watching her. Linnea lowered her gaze. "I'm surprised you buy pizza, being a Santoro and all."

Alex snickered. "We just don't tell Nonna. She'd be horrified."

"I bet she makes her own." Logan helped himself to the last piece. "Or is pizza some weird Americanization of real Italian food?"

"Our nonna is a curious mix. She was a young girl in Italy during the war years. Even though her memories are dark, nothing American is as good. It's wired in her that way." Jasmine reached for the jar of iced tea. "Anyone want another glass?"

Logan held out his. "It's really good. What is it?"

"Chamomile I found in an alley." She turned to Linnea. "You are planning a place for herbs in the community garden, aren't you?"

"For the butterflies and pollinators, yes."

"How about the people?"

Linnea dared crack a smile. "They can plant herbs in their own raised beds."

"Touché!" Alex raised his glass.

"Aw, come on. Tell me you're kidding. Think what a benefit a really large herb area would have for everyone. Nonna did tell you I want to put two beehives in the back corner, right?"

"Yes, she did. I need to look up the regs for that, though."

"I'm sure Eden would be happy to tell you," put in Logan. "She works for city animal control, after all."

Right, Logan's housemate had been dating Eden Andrusek for a few weeks now. Eden was a friend of Hailey's — enough reason for Linnea to steer clear even though Eden didn't seem as annoying.

"Good idea." Jasmine rose and set the empty pizza box by the door. "Hey, if you two have more time, do you want to take Linnea's truck over to Mom and Dad's for the living room set in the garage?" She looked from Alex to Logan and back again. "There's just a sofa, my papasan chair, and the desk. Anything else we can manage easily ourselves later."

"If Dermott isn't too tired." Alex stared at Logan, chin lifted.

"No problem there, unless they're too heavy for you, Santoro. I could call Jacob."

What a surprise neither bragged he could do it alone, one hand tied behind his back. Sending the two of them out unsupervised was probably not a good idea. Jasmine's smirk said she wasn't unaware. Okay then. Linnea handed her keys to Alex. He at least knew where his parents lived. She wasn't sure Logan did.

Alex's eyes gleamed with satisfaction. "Move it, Dermott."

The door closed behind the two men, and Linnea sank her flushed face into her hands.

A chair scraped back. Glasses clanked together as Jasmine gathered them.

Oh, no. Linnea sprang to her feet. This was her home, too. Her roomie shouldn't do all the work. "I'm sorry."

"Sorry for what, girl? Sorry for having two guys interested in you?" Jasmine set the glasses by the sink. "Although it's hard to remember my little brother is actually a grownup already."

Linnea gathered the plates. "I had no idea. I'm so embarrassed."

"Don't be. They tell me it's natural."

"But you don't have a boyfriend. Do you?"

Jasmine shook her head. "Not looking, either. No matter how many men Nonna parades past me." Her long hair hid her face as she turned on the faucet.

"Have you been... hurt?"

"Not like you think. There was someone, once, but it didn't work out. I'll get over it."

Was this something she should remember? Linnea had known the Santoros peripherally for several years, but

Jasmine was two years older than her and Alex, so they hadn't run in the same circles back then.

"You know why I asked you to room with me?" Jasmine glanced out from behind her curtain.

"Why?" Hopefully Jasmine hadn't changed her mind.

"A few reasons, none of them named Alex. One, I like you. We're both quiet, and we've gotten along well whenever we've connected. Two, I know you're a believer. And three, you seem in need of a friend."

Linnea swallowed hard. "Thank you. And yes, I need a friend. My parents..."

Jasmine rinsed a glass under the tap and set it upside down on a towel. "Tell me?"

"Nothing I ever do is good enough for my dad. It's like I'm still twelve."

"Why did you still live with them?"

Because she lacked the confidence to make a break? "He doesn't really pay me enough to get my own place. Don't worry. I can afford half of this." So long as she didn't get fired for insubordination.

The fourth glass joined the first three. Jasmine slid the plates into the suds. "Maybe you need a new job?"

"Maybe. I don't know. Thanks for taking a chance on me. I promise you won't regret it."

"I know I won't. I asked God to show me the right person to share a rental, and He led me straight to you."

Huh. Now she was the answer to someone's prayer? It shouldn't seem that strange. Jasmine was certainly the answer to one of hers. Whether either Logan or Alex was the answer to another remained to be seen.

Chapter 5

EYES CLOSED, LOGAN let the last few notes of the closing hymn drift from his fingertips.

Pastor Tomas gave the benediction into the hushed stillness that followed. Seconds later, the rustling and murmuring began as people gathered both belongings and children.

Logan wasn't ready for worship to be over. Wasn't ready to talk to anyone, which was unusual. He started through the closing hymn one more time, quieter this time. Tomas's sermon had pierced his heart today. Humility.

Some people — like Linnea — already had an overdose of that spiritual quality, but it was definitely not one Logan had ever sought for himself. He knew better than to wallow in pride, but seeking humility didn't appear to be the same thing as resisting pride.

How he'd treated Alex Santoro last night had been a lot closer to ego than to humility. Like Logan couldn't even let Linnea decide which of them suited her better. Like she'd automatically find the winner of the match to be the winner of her heart. He hadn't been egging Alex on simply to amuse himself no matter what he told himself. He fully intended to win.

And then what? Marry her? Because she didn't deserve to be fought over, won, and then deserted. That was beyond cruel, and Logan wasn't that kind of man. When he played for keeps, he meant the dictionary definition, which had nothing temporary about it.

Some women wouldn't take it seriously, but Linnea did. It was written in her blushes, in her trembling hands, in the fact that she hadn't come out of her bedroom when he and Alex returned with the furniture not half an hour later.

Humility. He needed to get serious about it. He'd work more of it out in front of the keyboard at home. No doubt Jacob would be off somewhere with Eden, leaving him a quiet place to think, something he usually avoided. Today it called.

The sanctuary was nearly empty when the last notes died away and he opened his eyes. A few people still chatted in the foyer, visible through the open doorway at the back. Logan laid the runner across the keys and lowered first the fallboard then the lid, nestling the prop in its space. A flip of the fitted quilted cover had most of it landing where it should. He straightened it and pushed the bench in.

Linnea was gone when he made it to the foyer. No surprise. How could she see past the macho male he'd tried — and failed — to portray last night? He'd be lucky if she spoke to him again. Except they were going to work together on the garden, so they'd both have to get over it or disappoint Marietta. A thwarted Italian grandmother wouldn't go away quietly.

He fingered his cell phone. Should he call her now, or would she still be so busy unpacking she wouldn't want to think about either him or Marietta? Maybe give her a day or two more.

"I didn't know if you were going to show up for work today." Dad rested his beefy arms on the side of the pickup truck box.

He'd made her wait all day for that? Linnea heaved the gas trimmer into the truck. "Why wouldn't I? I have a job." *As far as I know.*

"Thought you were maybe too good to work for your dad."

Her hands shook. She'd been waiting for his challenge. Working with a silent, glowering man all day had been unnerving, but she'd decided it was up to him to start the conversation. "I like what I do. You're stuck with me for a while yet."

"Humph." He turned away from the truck. "Don't forget to dump the clippings."

"No problem. I'll do it on my way..." *Home.* Yeah. No point saying that and rubbing salt in an open wound. It was going to take a while for her parents to get over this. But the fact was, even after two days and with all the furniture being Jasmine's, the apartment felt more like home than the house she'd lived in since she was fourteen.

Dad's truck peeled out of the Ridleys' circle drive, the clients they'd served on Mondays for as long as she'd had been working with him. Linnea gathered the remaining tools and drove out at a more leisurely pace.

Her phone rang. She glanced at it, face down on the passenger seat. No. If she'd been in the other truck she could've answered hands-free, but better not risk it while in motion. Still, she couldn't resist flipping it over to see who was calling.

Logan?

Her pulse quickened. She hadn't talked to him since Saturday evening when Jasmine had sent him and Alex for the sofa. She'd sat at the back during church and dashed out right after the closing prayer.

So she was chicken. She'd been a professional conflict-avoider her entire life. Logan seemed to like riling things up, so he was definitely someone she should steer clear of. If only she hadn't agreed to work with him on the garden. Maybe she should stop by Marietta's and... no. She'd moved out of her parents' house over this. She'd keep professional distance with Logan and get through the project as quickly as possible.

Her phone rang again.

She clenched the steering wheel. Had she bought everything she needed for supper? She and Jasmine had agreed to alternate Monday-Wednesday-Friday weeks with Tuesday-Thursday. She hadn't done a lot of cooking, so this was a good opportunity for practice. She couldn't go too far wrong with a stir-fry. She hoped.

Her phone chimed to alert her to a voicemail.

Logan probably felt the same way she did, that it was best to get this project started so it could get finished and they wouldn't have to work together anymore.

Right after supper she'd bring out her notebook and get started sketching the ideas that had been rattling around in her head since last week.

Linnea hadn't answered. She hadn't returned his call. He'd left a message. That had been two days ago.

Ouch. What was a guy supposed to do with that? Hadn't she been sending off go-away-Alex vibes? He'd only been trying to help. Okay, maybe a little more than that.

It burned to think she might prefer a kid like Santoro over him, but that was silly. She was friends with the family. Logan was a newcomer. Honestly, he was just cruising through and didn't know how to take anything seriously except the next vacation. So she was better off with Santoro. He'd be safer. Steadier.

Logan sat on the park bench by the basketball court, his tablet beside him, out of the way of his jiggling knee. Seemed like he'd sat there for hours before the Ranta Landscaping truck came around the corner and turned into the apartment parking lot. He stood and wiped damp hands down his khakis, dredged deep for his suave smile, and sauntered toward her, tablet under his arm.

Her long tanned legs, clad in denim shorts, swung out of the white truck, and the rest of her followed. She reached back to grab a backpack, which she swung over her shoulder as the door slammed shut and beeped.

As Logan closed the distance.

She looked good, no doubt about it. A navy tank top clung to her torso, and a wide-brimmed hat hid her eyes. That didn't prevent him from knowing when she saw him, though. Her steps faltered then speeded as though she could get up the steps and into the building before he reached the same spot.

Not happening. "Hi, Linnea!" He leaned against the wrought iron railing, all but blocking her entry.

"Um, hi." Her gaze darted to meet his then away. "Sorry. I've been working on the project, but I don't have anything definitive yet. I'll let you know when I do. Probably another week."

"I'm sorry, Linnea. I bungled things on Saturday. I didn't like..." Like what? How her best friend's brother, whom she'd probably known her entire life, looked at her? Alex hadn't been inappropriate. Logan spread his hands. "I'm not proud of the way I baited the..." Kid? Better not say that. "Baited Santoro. Alex."

Pink infused her cheeks in no time flat. "I was... uncomfortable."

"I know. I honestly am sorry."

She just looked at him for a long moment, her eyes nearly hidden in the shadow of her hat. "Okay."

Just like that? Over?

"But I'm really not finished with the garden plan. I wasn't lying to avoid you."

No, she'd been avoiding him in other ways. He held up his tablet. "Do you mind taking a few minutes to look over what I've done so far, to make sure we're on the same wavelength?"

Linnea looked at him uncertainly. "Jasmine won't be home. She's at her cousin's for dinner."

Didn't he have a few cousins on his dad's side? He couldn't remember ever meeting any, let alone getting a random dinner invite.

He smiled. "I'm free tonight, too. Why don't I go for some take-out and we can get our plans on the same page?

The garden plans, I mean." Duh. What other plans were there?

Her eyes didn't meet his. "Um, I guess. There's a picnic table over by the hoops. We could meet there in half an hour."

"You've got it." He saluted then jogged down two blocks' worth of metal stairs to the rental he shared with Jacob, drove to the nearest Chinese take-out and back to the picnic shelter, all the while worrying Linnea would stand him up.

But there she was, yellow pencil tucked behind her ear amid damp hair, flipping through a steno pad. Her job demanded fitness, so no wonder she was lean. That didn't keep her from being cute. Quite pretty, really.

He slid onto the bench beside her, setting the bags on the table. "Chinese, at your service."

"Sounds good. Thanks." She closed the notebook and pushed it to the side. "How do you and Jacob schedule meals?"

Logan opened the folding cardboard containers. Sweet-and-sour pork permeated his nostrils. Man, he was starving. "We usually alternate, more or less, but we're okay if plans change. Sometimes one of us works late, or has other plans." He shook his head. "Suddenly Jacob has other plans for the next month."

That got Linnea's attention. "What do you mean?"

"His boss sent him to Africa. Told him yesterday, and he leaves tomorrow."

"Wow, that's not much notice."

Logan scooped some chow mein, beef and greens, and pork balls onto a paper plate and set it in front of Linnea before loading his own. "No, it's not a lot, but he's done it enough times to know the drill. One of his coworkers was scheduled to go, but something came up. Mind if I ask the blessing?" He didn't wait, just launched into a quick prayer.

"You make it sound so everyday."

"You mean travel?" He glanced at her, captured by the sight of her with a fork halfway to her pursed pink mouth.

She nodded. "I haven't been anywhere further than Yellowstone and Disneyland. You?"

Whoa. Was that even possible in this millennium? "Yeah, I've been around some." He didn't want to sound like he was bragging.

"Like where?" She popped in the broccoli and chewed, watching him expectantly.

If he could keep the guarded expression away for a while, he'd play along. "I once spent three months backpacking through the Andes."

Her blue eyes widened. "Wow."

"I was escaping, to be honest. I didn't want to deal with North America anymore."

"I've wanted to escape a few times." Her voice was so low he wasn't sure he'd heard it.

"Where would you go?"

"I don't know. Mexico? Hawaii? But that's where everyone goes."

"That's how I felt, too. I craved adventures not everyone had. On the other hand, it was through missionaries I met at a campground in Argentina that I came to know Jesus, so even though I thought I was making my own choices, I have to believe God orchestrated my life behind the scenes."

Linnea stabbed a piece of ginger beef. "Sounds really cool. Where else have you been?"

"South America and Africa, most often. God has a purpose for my life, but I can't see the big picture. I try to take it one assignment at a time. I met Jacob through his brother-in-law, a guy who was instrumental in opening my eyes to the larger vision. Keanan's big thing is helping bring solar energy to rural Africa."

"Is that where he lives?"

"No, he lives at Green Acres Farm in northern Idaho. Not sure if you've heard of it."

Linnea shook her head. "I don't think so."

"It's a communal farm near Galena Landing. Both Jacob's sisters live there with their families and a bunch of other Christians. They grow most of their own food and have a school to teach farming to people. It's close enough for a day trip. Want to visit sometime? You'd probably love it."

"Maybe." But she didn't look convinced. "Why didn't you and Jacob move there?"

Logan chuckled. "Jacob's not much of a farm boy, which makes it ironic that he's dating Eden Andrusek. He does *not* like Eden's goat."

"Why not? I've been thinking of putting my name on the wait list for goat's milk. Pansy is cute."

"Who knows why Jacob Riehl thinks anything? Seems like we can plan things all we want, but sometimes people fall in love even when they didn't expect to." Somehow his gaze snagged on hers. "With someone they might not have thought was their perfect match. When they weren't even looking."

That couldn't be what was happening to him, could it? Wasn't his response to Linnea simply that of an alpha male protecting her from someone clearly unsuitable? But he'd been attracted to her even before Alex.

"Do you really think people can get over those things and live happily ever after?"

He turned and swung one leg over the bench, straddling it facing her. "Yeah, I really do." The big question at the moment was whether he was willing to go the distance himself.

She regarded him thoughtfully, as though analyzing the same thing.

Here went nothing. Logan reached for Linnea's free hand and ran his thumb across her wrist. "I'm not sure I believe in fairy tales, but I do think that if two people are attracted to each other, they should get to know each other and pray about it. God has a way of guiding those who are willing to let Him."

She bit her lip but didn't break eye contact.

Logan leaned a little closer. "As for happily-ever-after, there's probably a bit more work to it than that. But I've heard the results are truly worth the effort."

"No fairy tales, huh?" She studied his face.

"The real world is more interesting. Don't you think?"

"I-I'm not sure."

Chapter 6

ASMINE WAITED FOR HER outside Bridgeview Bakery and Bistro after work. "I'm sorry I made you eat alone last night. It wasn't fair of me so soon, but I haven't seen much of Francesca lately."

Linnea floated a few inches above the ground. "Oh, I didn't eat alone." She pulled the bakery door open.

Her roommate gave her a sharp look as she followed her inside. "Well, it wasn't Alex, being as he was lying on the floor with Tieri bouncing on his ribs while he built towers for little Luca to knock over. Did you have dinner with your parents?" Her eyes widened. "Wait... Logan?"

Linnea nodded, unable to wipe off the smile. "I'm sorry. I mean, I really like your brother. He's a good friend, but I just can't see ever falling in love with him." She clamped her mouth shut, feeling the all-too-familiar heat wash her face. "I'm not saying I'm in love with Logan. I barely know him."

"I understand. You're saying it's a possibility. That's cool." Jasmine waved at Kassidy North, one of the bakery's owners, who stood behind the counter. "Hi, Kass! Is there any way Linnea and I can put in a standing order for a dozen whole-grain cheese buns and a loaf of sourdough bread every week? We're rooming together in the Bridgeview Apartments."

Linnea followed Jasmine closer, eying the cases of sweets. Her mouth watered at the sight of the cinnamon rolls. "Maybe a dozen of those a week, too."

Jasmine looked at her with raised eyebrows.

Linnea shrugged. "We're both physically active at work. We can burn those off no problem."

"Are they that good?"

"Oh. Yeaaah."

Kass giggled. "Want to try one now?" She reached into the display case with a pair of tongs, grasped a roll, and set it on a plate. "Here you go."

Jasmine nudged Linnea's hand aside. "It's not for you."

"It's *what?*" Oh, the embarrassment.

"You've already tried them. This is to sell me." Jasmine laughed. "Okay, fine, I'll share with you. I was teasing."

"I knew that." And she kind of did, but the knowledge didn't cut the heat on her face.

Jasmine took a bite, and her eyes widened.

Linnea nodded. "Told you."

"Get out! Where have you and Hailey been hiding these things?"

"Right here." Kass pointed at the display case, her eyes dancing. "Like it?"

"*Like* it? I'm going to gain fifty pounds by Christmas eating these things." She took another bite and groaned. "But what a way to go."

Linnea passed over enough cash to pay for two and waited for Kass to hand her a second one. "Are you okay with standing orders, Kass? Or is it better if we take our chances?"

"They're perfect if you don't mind the baked goods frozen. It won't be more than a day or two in advance, but we don't bake every single thing every day."

"That's okay. We'll keep them frozen at the apartment, too, and just dole out the daily portions." Linnea laughed as Jasmine licked her fingers. "Otherwise we'd have cinnamon rolls one night for supper and then have no sweets for our lunches."

Kass dug out a notebook and jotted down the order. "We're getting more and more of these. What day works for pickup?"

Jasmine beat her to a reply. "Is Saturday okay? Then we're set for the upcoming week."

"Sure. Any time after eleven."

"Perfect. So we'll get a few cheese buns to tide us through the next few days. What do you have for deli meat?"

"We've been doing roasted chicken and ham this week. We're trying to get consistent local suppliers, but it hasn't been as easy as we'd hoped. Our needs are so specific."

Linnea and Jasmine exchanged a nod. "Some of each sounds good. I see you still have some gazpacho left from lunch." Linnea pointed at the tureen. "Mind if we each have a bowl while you slice meat?"

"No problem. There's just enough left for the two of you. Hailey will be glad not to face it again over supper. Figuring out how much to make of everything has been challenging."

"I bet." Linnea nodded. "I can't imagine having to plan in such detail. I like a bit of spontaneity at mealtime." Although having Mom cook hadn't been all bad. It had been more fun than being responsible for half of it herself.

Jasmine ladled the soup and pointed at a bistro table by the window with her chin.

Linnea sat down across from her. "Thanks." They'd figure out who owed what to whom at home. It seemed to work itself out.

Her roommate leaned across the table. "Okay, now I want details. How did it happen you went out for dinner with Logan last night?"

"Shh." Linnea glanced toward the serving area, but Kass had the meat slicer on. "We didn't go out, exactly. He caught me after work to invite me for Chinese, and we ate at the park while working on Marietta's design. So it really wasn't a date at all."

"You look awfully smug for someone who didn't have a date." Jasmine raised her eyebrows. "At all."

"We'll be working together on the garden for months in our spare time."

"Uh huh. The same thing was true last Saturday."

Behind the counter, Hailey conferred with Kass and tossed them a wave.

Linnea wasn't sure how to respond to the woman with a blatant crush on the man who'd indicated he wanted to get to know Linnea better.

Jasmine waved back then refocused on Linnea. "So what did he say?" She lowered her voice. "And don't tell me about Marietta's garden. Puh-leeze. Tell me what he said that got the sparkle in your eye."

"Okay." Linnea took a deep breath and let it out. "Logan invited me to go to the Spokane Indians ballgame against Boise on Saturday!"

"Seriously?" Jasmine's eyes grew wide. "Wow, that's not half bad for a first date. How did he know you love baseball? I hope he's already got the tickets, because I heard they're sold out."

Linnea grinned. "I know, right? I'll be honest. He didn't buy them with me in mind. He and his roommate were going to go, but Jacob's boss sent him to Africa. I don't mind being second choice for a baseball game. At least it's not because some other woman turned him down or something weird like that."

"I'm stoked for you, girl. He seems like a great guy. Just don't go getting married right away and leave me without a roommate. Deal?"

Getting married? Linnea's insides fluttered. Surely she'd scare Logan off long before that became a real question. But, for now, she'd enjoy having a boyfriend and, like Logan said, pray for God's leading and blessing. "I don't think you have to worry about that anytime soon."

"I've got your items ready whenever you are," Kass said from over at the counter. "No rush. I'll lock the doors and start the cleanup routine while you girls finish."

Hailey must already be cleaning back in the kitchen.

"Oh, sorry! We'll be out of your way in just a minute."

Logan couldn't believe this was the same woman. Linnea had pulled her ponytail through the hole at the back of a red Spokane Indians ball cap and jumped up and down beside him wearing a replica jersey.

He liked a good ballgame as well as any red-blooded American male, especially a game tied at the bottom of the seventh like the one currently playing out in front of them in Avista Stadium, but he hadn't expected this. Hadn't expected *her.*

"Run! Run! Run!" screamed Linnea. A second later she dropped to the bleachers beside him. "Nooo. Did you see that? He was safe."

"You're something else."

She looked at him, clearly confused. "You think the ump was right?"

Logan grinned. "I have no idea."

"But—" A shrill whistle from the diamond broke through her words. She pivoted to face the game, both hands pressed against her mouth.

"Batter *up!*"

The Boise pitcher massaged the ball, staring down the man wearing Spokane whites. A fiery windup then the ball arrowed across the plate. The batter swung. Missed.

Linnea let out a squeak. Only her eyes moved with the ball. Another strike before the batter connected with a sharp *thwack*, sending the ball low down the third baseline while he tore toward first.

The fielder snagged the ball after one bounce and hurled it at first base with the speed of a pitch. The ball slammed into the baseman's mitt as the runner dove for the base.

Safe? Out?

The Jumbotron flashed the message the instant the umpire signaled. Safe.

Linnea dropped to the bleachers and covered her face. "I can't look. Tell me what happens next."

Logan bit back a laugh. It wasn't the ballgame that riveted his attention. It was the conundrum of the woman beside him. He'd thought she'd accepted the invitation because of him. Well, reality ought to take him down a peg or two. She barely remembered who was beside her.

"Strike!"

Linnea peeked between her fingers, then hung her head between her knees.

He nudged her. "Praying?" Probably some thought ballgame results were worth begging God about. He'd always considered sports great entertainment. Maybe he'd moved too often to have deep affinity for any one team.

"Strike!"

Linnea groaned without looking up. "Nooo."

"It's just a game." He peeled her long fingers away from her face. They were stronger than they looked.

She glared at him and clasped her hands in her lap. "How can you even say that?"

Logan massaged her fingers between his own. "Whether Spokane wins or loses, the sun will still rise tomorrow." He kept his voice teasing. "Breezes will still drift along the river."

Her eyes softened. "Heresy," she whispered. "How can you speak such nonsense when the fate of the universe is being decided down on the diamond this very minute?"

"Really? The entire universe? Right here? Right now?" She was rocking his. And the realization rocked it further.

Linnea nodded slightly. "It's not just a game. Not just a show."

He held his finger across her lips. "There's more than one show going on here." He wouldn't even have this much of her attention if the Spokane Indians weren't jogging across the infield.

She scanned the diamond as though looking for a circus act.

"You." She hadn't seemed to notice his finger, so he slid it across her cheek and back again.

This time her blue eyes focused on his and widened. The telltale flush got started. "You... You're watching me?"

"I am." He took the liberty to cradle her jaw with his palm.

Linnea swallowed hard. "But there's a game."

"I know." He leaned a little closer. "But you are far more interesting. Just when I think I have a vague idea what makes you tick, I find out I didn't have a clue."

"But you're the one who invited me."

"Pure luck the first time." Logan lowered his voice. "I had no idea I was giving you your heart's desire."

"My heart..." Her words trailed into the minuscule space between them.

"Next time it will be on purpose. If you'll come with me again." Logan swept his lips across hers.

Linnea froze, blue eyes super-glued to his.

The wonder in her eyes gave her away. She'd never been kissed before, not even a gentle brush. He hadn't meant anything by it — had he? — but his impetuousness robbed her of the possibility of a proper first kiss by someone who was firmly committed to a future with her.

Linnea was a sheltered flower. A butterfly just emerging from her chrysalis with damp, fragile wings. She deserved someone with more depth than he had. With more compassion and endurance.

He hadn't set out to hurt her, but it was inevitable all the same.

Chapter 7

AD WOULD FLIP if he saw her sitting under Marietta's grape arbor with a goblet of wine, but the old woman hadn't asked if she wanted any. Just told Ray to pour a glass for each of them as though Linnea had already said yes.

Beside her, Logan tipped his glass toward Ray and Marietta. "*Grazie.*"

"Yes, thank you." She set her drink on the shelf of the short statue beside her. Maybe no one would notice if she sort of forgot it there.

Ray leaned back in his chair and had a sip as he looked between her and Logan. "Mamma says you have made good plans for the garden. May I see?"

Logan handed a tube of drawings to the older man. "We're very excited about the opportunities. It's a good space and should serve the neighborhood well. Thank you, Marietta. It's a generous gift to the community."

The guy was slick.

Ray unrolled the plans onto a low glass table between them, anchoring the edges with the wine bottle, a small plant, and a hand trowel. He traced the rectangles with his finger and glanced at Linnea. "A step up for every two beds?"

She nodded. "The slope distance isn't great. Adding sixteen inches vertically for every fourteen linear feet works well. That's two four-foot beds and two three-foot walkways."

"And a six-foot walkway up the center. The beds are sixteen-footers? So that's thirty-eight wide, and the lot is ninety."

"Jasmine suggested a perennial area for herbs and berries. That's the purpose of the lengthwise beds up against Marietta's fence."

Ray chuckled. "That's my girl. And I see you've marked off a corner for her beehives. You've checked the city regulations?"

"Yes, Jasmine asked Eden Andrusek for input. Eden works for animal control and helped us design the hedge here." Linnea pointed at the curve on the paper. "She also suggested a separate water source in their area so there's less likelihood of bees in the birdbath. We don't want anyone stung."

Logan leaned in, the heat of his arm brushing Linnea's. "We're building a temporary fence around the hives until the hedge grows up and fills in."

Ray glanced up. "How tall?"

"Six feet minimum."

He shook his head. "For how many hives?"

"Two."

"This is crazy. Mamma, why are you encouraging Jasmine?"

"Pollinators. They will be busy little bees." The old woman looked smugly around her backyard oasis where tomatoes of many varieties had begun to ripen.

Ray chuckled. "Then why only two?"

"City rules for the lot size," put in Linnea.

"But two hives are hardly worth the work and expense."

Marietta glared at him. "You will like the honey on your bread. On your struffoli. Say no more."

He raised both hands in good-natured defeat.

Whew. Linnea had been prepared to fight for the hives, but having Marietta as defender was better. Much better. It wasn't as though space was limited.

"I'm surprised some developer hasn't snapped up that lot already." Logan gestured beyond Marietta and Ray.

Marietta harrumphed.

Ray pointed at his mother. "She wouldn't sell. They offered good money. There once was a house there, a big one, that my father's parents had built. My parents lived there as newlyweds. It burned to the ground before I was born."

"The lot belongs to the Santoros. To Bridgeview." Frowning, Marietta tapped the paper. "It is not for some outside developer to build condos like he said." She said *condos* as though it were a dirty word.

Condos had their place. Much as Linnea loved outdoor areas, she got that whole thing about the plumber's leaky toilet and the shoemaker's barefoot children. Would she have been so eager to work for Dad if they'd had anything but patchy grass at their house? A condo didn't sound so bad. Someone else could take care of her own tiny yard after hours.

"We can't have that," murmured Logan.

She couldn't tell if he really agreed with Marietta or was being cheeky. With him, it was hard to know for sure. After that one heart-stopping moment at the ballgame last weekend, he'd pulled back to the guarded flirtation she'd experienced before. Same as he offered Jasmine. Same as the singles after church, other than Hailey. Yes, he probably spent more time with Linnea than anyone else — even more than Peter at the basketball court — but only because he was bored with his housemate away. The garden offered a diversion. When the carpentry parts were done, he'd drift on to some other project. Some other, more interesting, woman.

Marietta jabbed at the paper. "And here?" She squinted at Linnea.

Linnea sucked in air. "We were thinking a water feature."

"Oh?"

She cast a glance at Logan, but he leaned back and sipped his wine, smiling at her. Great. He was making her deal with the old woman. "A small pond with a waterfall and a pump. Logan says Jacob's company has solar pumps that can easily handle the volume, so we wouldn't have to run wiring." She looked between Marietta and Ray. "Trickling water is soothing."

"Laws require a fence if there's standing water, don't they?" Ray scratched his chin. "Not sure we want to get into the liabilities of a pond."

"There will be a fence around the whole lot," pointed out Logan. "Isn't that enough?"

"It has to be a certain height, though, and kept locked. Mamma was thinking of a regular picket fence." Ray held his hand a few feet above the patio pavers. "Low enough to see over and be inviting."

Marietta's mouth twitched one way then the other. "I hadn't thought of water, other than for plants."

"We could do a fountain in a pebble pond instead." Linnea pulled out her steno pad and drew a quick sketch. "Then there isn't enough standing water to be any danger, but there would still be moving water plus shallows for birds and butterflies."

"I can see little Santoro kids running through that to cool off." Ray grinned and nudged his mother. "Wouldn't shallow water be in danger of quick evaporation, though?"

"There are ways to automate water levels." Logan waved his hand. "Do either of you have any questions about the layout? Anything Linnea or I missed, or put in the wrong location?"

Linnea held her breath while Ray and his mom stared thoughtfully at the plans then glanced at each other.

"How many dollars will this cost?"

She handed over the envelope containing several sheets of paper detailing all the expenses she and Logan had come up with, but not wages. She bit her lip as Ray leaned over his mother's shoulder, their eyes roving over the columns.

Finally, Ray leaned back and nodded. "Looks good to me. I'll cut you a check to get started. If you need a place to store tools or supplies, feel free to use the shed on my property. I'll let Grace know you may be coming and going."

Logan leaned across the glass coffee table and shook Ray's hand. "Thank you. It will be a good project."

"Yes, thanks." Why couldn't she feel that confidence Logan emanated? She was the one in charge. Theoretically, anyway.

"Looks like you will be putting in a lot of hours. Keep track of those, won't you? I know Mamma asked you to volunteer, but..." Ray glanced at Marietta. "I think this goes beyond what we expected. We'll make sure there's compensation one way or another."

A knot inside Linnea loosened while another tightened. This was a terrific opportunity to develop her abilities, but it also meant months of free time spent with Logan. Whether that was a good thing or a bad thing remained to be seen.

"We did it!" Logan held up his hand for her high five. They stood on Marietta's front step, each with a signed contract and check.

She smacked his hand but didn't meet his gaze.

"Hey." He nudged her. "Aren't you happy?"

"Sure am!"

Logan followed her down to the main sidewalk. What was going on inside Linnea's mind? "Want to celebrate?"

She hesitated. "I should do some laundry."

"Laundry?" He couldn't help the laugh.

Her face reddened.

"Sorry. But seriously? We just scored a pretty sweet job. Want to go out to Frank's Diner? I'll get you home in plenty of time to get your clothes washed." If she was for real.

Linnea shot him a glance.

Aha, he was winning. "Or we could grab take-out from Bridgeview Bakery."

"Why?"

"Why what?"

"Why do you want to spend more time with me? I thought you'd need a break by now."

He reached for her hand, but it disappeared behind her back. "I like being with you. I thought maybe you felt the same." What did he have to go on, though? She only came alive when they were focused on the garden project. Or at the ball game.

Linnea shook her head and started down the sidewalk.

Logan fell into step beside her. He'd be more concerned if her cheeks weren't still blazing pink.

"There are lots of girls in Bridgeview that are prettier than me. More fun than me. You don't need to—"

"Linnea?"

"What?"

This wasn't in the script. She was supposed to play along and see what happened, not push him toward someone else. This hard-to-get routine after he'd seen promising signs messed with his mojo. He couldn't treat her like just anyone else. She was too fragile for that. He'd never broken anyone's heart that he knew of, and he'd rather not start now. But how could he boost her self-confidence without pretending there was more?

Maybe there *was* more.

Or maybe love was just in the air. Seeing Jacob come in every day from spending time with Eden — wow. His housemate had jumped in the game full-on. But then Jacob was a different temperament than Logan. He didn't do anything by halves. He didn't hold back when he made a decision.

The thing was, Jacob had never been in love before. Not even in *like*. Logan had been in love, if he could call it that, a dozen times. Maybe he didn't have the personality to commit to one woman for life, but Linnea didn't deserve to be hurt.

The signed contract wedged in his pocket, pressing against his hip. He could start right now by asking Linnea to find someone else to do the construction. He could walk away. Tomorrow would be too late.

"Logan?" Linnea stopped in the middle of the sidewalk, thumbs hooked through her belt loops, her head tilted to one side. "What's going on?"

It was already too late. She was beautiful in her jean shorts and pink tank. Her long blond hair swung loose today under her wide-brimmed hat. She might think Hailey or Jasmine or one of the others were prettier. She was wrong.

His mouth went dry, and he swallowed. "If I'd rather spend time with someone else, I'd have asked her. I asked you, Linnea."

You're the one.

He'd managed not to say that out loud, hadn't he? He'd teased Jacob for being so sure, so soon — although it would be interesting to see what would happen when his housemate realized Eden's goat was playing for keeps as well.

Linnea didn't have a goat. She didn't have anything holding her back that Logan couldn't embrace. She was shy, but that was nothing more tickets to Spokane Indians' ballgames wouldn't cure.

He held his hand toward her, but she didn't reach back. Just studied him from serious blue eyes.

"I have to go talk to my dad about using the Bobcat on Saturday," she said at last. She turned and strode away.

Logan caught her arm and fell in step with her. "Can I come with you?"

A rosy dot rode high on her cheekbone. "My dad's not going to like you."

That's what she thought. "Nearly everyone likes me."

"He won't."

"It sounds like you don't trust me. I can play nice." He twined his fingers with hers.

"I'm his baby, Logan. He was livid when I moved out of the house, not that I precisely asked permission. Still, moving in with Jasmine Santoro made the situation bearable. If he thinks there's a guy... interested... in me, he'll go ballistic."

"Linnea, there *is* a guy interested in you. And I don't want to hide that from your parents. I can't see how that could end well."

"It's too soon, Logan. Way too soon." She pulled her hand away from his. "You'll probably change your mind by next week, so there's no point in mentioning it."

She thought he was that fickle? She hadn't seen Logan Dermott in action yet, when he really wanted something. But was he actually falling in love with her, or was he only determined because she seemed resolved to put him off?

Logan snapped his mouth shut. He wasn't sure. And if he made a big deal about it, working together was going to be extremely awkward. That garden would consume a lot of evenings and weekends. He had time to win her over slowly.

Because he wasn't the kind to give up when the going got tough.

Chapter 8

LINNEA STOOD, HANDS DEEP in her pockets, while Dad drove the Bobcat down off the trailer. One last try. "Thanks. I can take it from here."

He glared at her before chugging to the first set of stakes. He set the blade and carved a path across the gently sloping lot.

So this was how it was going to be. Not content to merely disapprove, he'd keep pretending she was incompetent. She was perfectly capable of terracing the lot herself. But no, on top of his complaints about her moving out and taking on a volunteer project, now he was helping. Not for the sake of the project, but one more way to exercise his control over her.

Well, she could pretend this had been her plan all along. It was easier than arguing with a man driving equipment. She grabbed pegs, twine, and a measuring tape from her own truck — hers until Dad demanded it back — and began staking out the wildlife garden along the west edge of the lot.

Lavender, verbena, asters, daisies. Milkweed. In her mind she could already see the lush banks of blossoms with buzzing bees and fluttering butterflies. The lone lilac had become the inspiration for a lilac hedge along the fence, adding a windbreak for fragile wings.

The grinding gears as the Bobcat moved back and forth behind her provided an audible backdrop as she laid out curving beds and imagined gray stone paths into the heart of the flowers.

"Hey."

Who? What? Linnea whirled.

Logan stood a few feet away, his easy grin looking a bit forced. Or she might be imagining that part. "What's going on?"

Oh, no. She'd hoped by choosing to come so early on Saturday morning, she'd miss this moment. The one where he realized her daddy was going to rescue her. The one where he introduced himself to Dad, because she had no intention of doing it.

"My father decided to pitch in. And I'm laying out the beds."

She watched Logan's face as he processed. He glanced behind him at the Bobcat then back at her. "Nice of him."

If that's how Logan wanted to spin it. She offered all the smile she could muster, which wasn't much. "I wasn't expecting to see you here this morning."

He stepped closer. "Linnea—"

"Don't. Please." Had Dad seen? Not likely. The machine was edging away from them. "It's not like there's anything you can do at this stage."

Logan narrowed his gaze. "I can help you until the load of fencing material arrives." He glanced at his watch. "In about an hour."

He'd done the same as her, trying to get a head start without consulting the other.

"But..."

It was too late. The Bobcat spun a 180 at the end of the terrace then idled. Dad swung out of the small cab. Strode toward them.

Linnea tried to moisten her dry mouth and failed. "Run into trouble?" she asked Dad. Maybe it was all about the job, not about her. Not about the fact that a cute young man was talking to her.

Dad stopped beside Logan, his gaze twitching between the two of them while his hands flexed at his sides. "I don't know. Did I run into trouble?"

"Dad, I'd like you to meet Logan Dermott. Marietta conscripted him to do the carpentry on the project. Logan, this is my dad, Dave Ranta Senior."

"A carpenter, huh?" Dad's gaze lingered on Logan's shoulder-length hair before slowly taking in the rest of him.

"I am, sir." Logan rocked on his heels. "Pleased to meet you, Mr. Ranta."

"See that you keep to carpentering."

"Dad!" Heat exploded across Linnea's face.

"He's just a puppy, Linnea. Someday you'll meet a real man."

What, someday when she was thirty? Forty? She didn't dare look at Logan. She'd warned him Dad wouldn't like him, but even she hadn't expected this kind of rudeness. Maybe that was better than an explosion.

"Your daughter is an intelligent woman, Mr. Ranta. You've taught her to make good judgment calls. I don't think you need to worry about her."

Oh, Logan. Don't even start.

"I'm warning you." Dad swung back to Logan. "Keep your mitts off my daughter." Dad stood at least six inches taller and out-massed Logan by probably fifty pounds. He ran his hand over his buzz cut.

"Your daughter is worthy of respect. I would never take advantage of her."

Oh, where was a hole to crawl into? Just when she'd hoped to spread her wings, even a little, the chrysalis hardened even more.

"If you stay away from her, that won't be a problem." Dad's puffed-out chest nearly touched Logan's chin. "I can get someone to help her with the building parts here."

"I'm sorry you feel that way, sir. Linnea and I have already signed a contract with Marietta Santoro and her son Ray. I consider it an honor to work under your daughter's guidance. She's drawn up great plans for this lot, and I look forward to doing my part to make them a reality." He stared up into Dad's eyes, not seeming in the least intimidated. "With her."

Dad sighed. "Linnea, enough of this nonsense."

Lord, please help me. "Logan's right, Dad. We've both signed contracts to complete this garden."

"But they're not even paying you."

This wasn't the time to speculate on what Ray had meant about compensation. "A contract is still a contract. Logan is a friend of mine, and we're both committed to seeing this through."

Dad's eyebrows shot up. "Where did you pick up a *friend* like this?"

"We met at church. We know a lot of the same people." Well, Jasmine, at least. Linnea had been too shy to get to know the other young women much. Some of them seemed to have been friends forever, like Eden and Hailey. Eden seemed nice enough. Who knew why she hung out with Hailey?

"Church." Dad made it sound like a swear word. "And here I thought church was all about boys looking like boys."

Logan didn't look any less masculine for the length of his hair. Maybe it even had helped attract her to him, as it proved how different he was from her family. Linnea allowed herself to drink in the sight of him even now. There was nothing unmanly about him. He didn't exude the same power her dad did, but that wasn't masculinity so much as bullying.

Really? Dad a bully?

Linnea straightened and met Logan's gaze before turning back to her father. "Would you prefer me to finish the terracing, Dad? Logan reminded me that the fencing material will be here in less than an hour, and it would be nice if the leveling were done before it arrived."

Dad glared at her. "I said I'd do it, and I will."

She turned to Logan. "Can I get a hand with the exact location of the pebble pond? Did Ray show you where the water main enters the property?"

Her father bristled and opened his mouth. After a few seconds, he blustered off and climbed back on the Bobcat. The engine growled.

Every muscle in Linnea's body trembled as she turned away. She sensed Logan stepping up beside her.

"I'm sorry to come between you and your dad."

"I tried to tell you."

"I'll pray for you both. God can soften hearts."

Whether he meant Dad's or hers, she didn't know. Maybe time would tell.

Meeting Linnea's father certainly gave Logan something to think about as the Bobcat bit into the slope behind him over and over. He tried to focus on pounding in pegs where Linnea indicated while aware of the man's eyes boring into him. Had someone painted a large red X on his back? It felt like it.

Show respect, not fear.

Yeah, Mr. Ranta had rattled him as few men ever had. And he didn't need to dig too far to figure why this moment was different. The desire to protect Linnea welled from a place deep within him. A new sensation.

The Bobcat's gears ground as it rolled toward the street. Logan dared a glance. Linnea's dad drove the machine up the ramp and onto the low-bed trailer. He then strapped the Bobcat into place and hopped down.

"Looks good, Dad," Linnea called out. "Thank you."

"Your mother is expecting you for supper."

Linnea hesitated. "Sorry, I won't be able to make it today. She can give me a call and we'll set up another day."

Good girl.

Mr. Ranta pointed a finger in their direction. "Watch yourself." He jumped into the cab of his pickup and rumbled down the street.

Linnea sank to the rough ground. "I'm sorry you had to witness that."

"It's okay. I understand things better now." Like scales had fallen off his eyes.

She plucked a handful of grass. "He means well."

He settled cross-legged in front of her, knees touching hers. "Do you think so?" Man, he was no psychologist, but her father reeked of self-absorption, not true love.

"Of course. He's my dad."

"Linnea, I don't want to come between you and him. I really don't. But from here, it looks like he's manipulating you."

The telltale flush crept up her cheeks. "Of course he is protective. I'm his only daughter. The baby of the family."

"He doesn't know how to let go."

She closed her eyes. "Too true."

Logan gathered both her hands in his. "How does it make you feel?"

"Trapped," she whispered. "Maybe that's why I love butterflies so much. They at least can break out and fly away."

"No cocoon is forever." He stroked her trembling hands with his thumbs. "At least not if the butterfly wants to be free."

"I'm being silly." A lone tear wandered down her cheek, but wiping it away would require releasing her.

"You're not." Logan squeezed her hands. "May I pray for you?"

"I'd appreciate it."

"Dear Lord, I lift Linnea up to You. You know her heart is hurting, and I pray that You will restore it. I pray that You'll work in her dad so he'll be open to You and able to bless Linnea to be the woman You created her to be." *What part am I playing in this transformation, Lord?* "We turn this situation over to You, trusting You to work things out to the best for those who love You, for those who are called according to Your purpose. Lord, You've called Linnea to be Your child. You've called me, as well. Thank You. Please give us the faith to trust You in this situation. In Jesus' name, amen."

He peeked at Linnea. That first tear had been followed by several more. He couldn't stand it. His thumb reached up and gently wiped the rivulet away. "Linnea?"

"I didn't know you meant right now."

"Meant what?" His mind scrambled to catch up. "To pray for you?"

She nodded, and he cupped her face between both hands. "I've been praying for you for a couple of weeks now. I'm just thankful to have this opportunity to pray *with* you. You're never far from my thoughts, Linnea. And my thoughts often become a prayer."

"How do you do that?" she whispered.

"The Bible says to pray without ceasing. I don't think it means to always verbalize a formal prayer, but rather being aware that God is with us all the time and loves to hear from us. To be remembered and included as part of each passing moment."

"You must have been raised in a Christian home."

If only. Logan shook his head. "My family doesn't understand any more than your father does."

That got her attention. Her eyes popped open and she focused on his. "Really?"

"Yeah. My mom is a serial monogamist. My two younger sisters and I all have different fathers. I got shuffled back and forth between parents when I was a kid and struck out on my own when I was sixteen. I just couldn't hack it anymore."

"What happened then? I can't imagine."

Logan shrugged. "There are parts best forgotten. I drifted around doing odd jobs and eventually found that, not only was I good with a hammer, I could find temporary work nearly anywhere. I became interested in food security—"

"What's that?"

He snorted. "That's what this country doesn't have. We're dependent on transporting food around the world. Who even knows what time of year bananas are supposed to be ripe? Or asparagus? We demand our grocery stores carry the same produce year around. We don't care where it comes from or how expensive it is to get it here or whether it tastes any good when it does."

Her eyes widened. "I've been thinking about stuff like that. The veggies at the farmers' market taste so much better than anything in the store. But what do you mean by security?"

Logan knew he'd liked this woman for a reason. Possibly more than one. "I mean that if something went wrong, we don't have a good local supply of food. Nobody does. We depend on trading with other countries. We depend on ships and planes and trucks being able to access anything anytime. Wars in the Middle East revolve around oil to maintain our current lifestyle, but food is an even bigger trigger and so often ignored."

"So that's what Marietta is doing." Linnea waved at the rough terraces off to the side. "Making it easier for people to grow their own food. But we have serious winter here. What grows then?"

He grinned. "That's what canning is for. Freezing. Dehydrating. Our ancestors did it. We can do it, too. Lots of people are trying to relearn the old ways before they're lost."

"I had no idea."

"I told you about Green Acres Farm in northern Idaho, right? Where Jacob's sisters live?"

Linnea nodded.

"They're totally into this food security thing. They grow nearly all of their own food and teach others how. A lot of people want to make a difference. They're actually doing it."

"That sounds really interesting."

The truck delivering fencing supplies chose that moment to pull up at the curb. Logan surged to his feet, pulling Linnea up with him. "We'll find a day and go visit, okay?"

Suddenly it seemed important to introduce her to his friends. What would they think of her?

Chapter 9

"SIT WITH ME?" Logan leaned close in the foyer before church on Sunday.

Wasn't that like announcing they were dating? Linnea had seen all the speculative looks when Jacob and Eden began sitting together in church. Wait, were she and Logan dating? They'd certainly spent a lot of time together in the past week at the garden site.

Across the foyer, Hailey's eyes gleamed as they caught sight of Logan then narrowed when focusing on Linnea. What was this, junior high? Could Hailey really not clue in that Logan had no interest in her?

Maybe she just couldn't believe Linnea had anything she didn't. That was probably it, and no wonder. Hailey was pretty and poised and perfectly proportioned. Unlike Linnea.

Logan's hand cupped her elbow. "Please?"

"You just want to be rescued from Hailey."

His eyes twinkled. "Not *only*. I'm playing this morning, and I want to sit beside you when I'm not up front."

A practically front-row seat for Logan's piano playing? Tempting. "People are going to think..."

"I hope they do."

Seriously? They were having this conversation minutes before church? He'd been hinting toward it all week, though. He'd been awesome. Supportive but not pushy. This was borderline pushy.

She found herself in motion, his hand under her elbow propelling her toward the front of the church. Resistance would make even more of a scene. "There's Jasmine and Alex," she murmured. "There's room."

Logan squeezed her arm and leaned so close her senses filled with his aftershave and warmth. "No ditching me for Alex."

Heat swept up her face as she edged in beside Jasmine.

"Save me a spot," he said loud enough for Alex to hear as he set his Bible on the aisle seat then headed for the piano.

A moment later he looked lost in the music as he played *It is Well with My Soul*.

Peace like a river. Linnea breathed it in. She needed to quit worrying about everything all the time.

"Things okay?" whispered Jasmine.

Linnea smiled and nodded, joining in singing the words. One worship song led to another and, before she knew it, Logan was nestled into the seat beside her with Pastor Tomas on the platform.

Afterward, she had no idea what the sermon had been about. She'd been way too distracted by Logan's arm and leg wedged against hers. What were people thinking? What was Alex thinking? She shouldn't be so relieved her parents didn't come to church. Something about that seemed wrong. *Was* wrong. She shouldn't have sat beside Logan. He hadn't given her a lot of options, but she hadn't used the one she had, that of simply saying no.

As the closing notes of the final hymn faded away, Alex leaned past Jasmine. "You could've said something."

Jasmine elbowed her brother. "Oh, leave her alone, Alex. It's not like you've spent the last six years chasing her."

"What do you know about it?" He narrowed his gaze at Jasmine.

Linnea frowned. "You were chasing me?"

He had the grace to blush. "I was working up to it. Getting established in my career."

She'd had no idea. "I don't know what to say."

"Say you'll ditch that guy." Alex jerked his chin toward Logan, who was in the process of closing up the baby grand. "Date me instead."

"Oh, Alex." Jasmine rolled her eyes. "How to make a girl feel loved."

"I'm no good at this stuff. If I were, we wouldn't be in this predicament."

Linnea stood and smoothed down her lime green skirt. "We're not in a predicament, Alex. You've been my friend forever, but I'm not in love with you. Please. Can we just forget about this?"

Logan's aftershave wafted over her as her back warmed from his nearness. "Forget about what?"

Heat flushed her face. "Nothing. Let's go."

"Linnea, you're making a mistake." Alex stretched a hand toward her but let it fall before he touched her. "He's not serious about you." He glanced toward Hailey, Eden, and their friends, who were making their way to the back of the sanctuary. "He's just using you to avoid Hailey North."

That wasn't right. Was it?

Logan chuckled. "While you're entirely correct that I'm trying to stay under Hailey's radar, you're badly mistaken if you think I'm using Linnea for that means." His hand caressed Linnea's hip, something he'd never done before. "I'm capable of simply telling someone I'm not interested." His hand slid up to her waist and back down. "Or of telling someone that I am. For instance, I'm very interested in Linnea. I find her endlessly fascinating. She has great ideas, she works tirelessly, and she's got a sense of humor that pops out when I least expect it. No, I'm definitely not using Linnea for any ulterior motives. I think she's terrific, and I enjoy spending time with her."

Linnea closed her mouth. She couldn't imagine her cheeks getting any hotter if she sat under a heat lamp.

Alex's chin jutted up. "I want to hear it from Linnea."

Jasmine jabbed his ribs. "Alex! She already told you she's not interested in you."

He crossed his arms. "She didn't tell me what she thinks of Dermott."

Linnea caught Logan's hand against her hip and leaned back against him slightly. "It's early days, Alex. Logan and I are spending time together, and we'll see how things work out. We're a long way from making a permanent commitment."

She couldn't believe she'd had to be that blunt with Alex, and in front of Logan, yet. How was she supposed to define their relationship? And why did she have to?

Logan leaned closer and rested his cheek against hers from behind. "Ready to go, babe?"

So it *was* possible to be redder than a minute ago. Who knew? "Um, sure." She grabbed her Bible and purse off the pew, not daring to meet Jasmine's gaze, and especially not Alex's. Or Logan's, for that matter.

He kept his hand curved around her hip as they made their way to the church door. Finally, they stepped into the outdoors, where the sun shone down from a bright blue sky and a gentle breeze lifted off the Spokane River.

Linnea stepped out of Logan's gentle grip. "It's okay." She glanced at him between lowered lashes.

He tipped his head. "What's okay?"

"You don't need to pretend."

Logan pressed his hand over his heart. "I am not pretending. There was nothing in my speech there simply to show up Santoro. Linnea, you *are* a beautiful woman, and I enjoy being with you. Like right now. I want to spend all day with you and get to know you better. Do you have a place around here that means a lot to you? Would you show it to me?"

"Really?"

He grasped both her hands. "Please?"

She nodded slowly, lost in his intense blue eyes. "Have you ever been to Manito Park?"

"No, but I hear it is on today's agenda."

"This is amazing." Logan slipped his arm around Linnea as they stood on the bridge over Kiri Pond in the Japanese garden section. "I can't believe the size of those koi."

A waterfall tumbled into the pond behind them, barely rippling either the surface or the muted sounds.

"It's my favorite spot in Manito, next to the butterfly garden."

"I can see why. It's so tranquil." A Japanese maple spread branches sprouting feathery red leaves across the pond. They weren't the only ones enjoying the space, but everyone seemed to respect the meditative ambience. "Have you ever designed a garden with these elements?"

Linnea was silent for so long he turned her to face him, looping both hands around her waist.

She glanced at him. "I haven't really designed any other spaces."

"Really? Marietta's lot is your first? It's going to look fantastic. I wouldn't have thought of using native stone instead of decorative concrete blocks, but I see where you got the idea from." Gray basalt outcroppings had been left throughout Manito by the park developers in the early twentieth century, yet plenty also edged walkways and created the park's headquarters and other buildings.

Linnea bit her lip. "Dad does the bit of designing we do. I'm the grunt."

Logan tipped her chin up to capture her gaze. "He's missing a terrific resource. Have you ever thought of starting your own business?"

That got her attention. "Me? I couldn't."

"Why not? I'd hazard a guess that when news of Marietta's garden gets around, you'll find yourself in demand."

"But Dad..."

"Dad what?" he pressed gently.

She shook her head. "It doesn't matter. It's not going to happen."

"It could." He leaned back against the bridge rail and drew her closer. "Be the butterfly, Linnea. Stretch your wings. Fly."

Her lips parted, and her eyes locked onto his.

Logan's breath hitched. Yes? No? Go for it or not? He tightened his hands on her back, pressing her against him. He slid one hand up into her thick blond hair. "Linnea?" he whispered.

She said nothing, but her gaze darted to his lips then back to his eyes.

He'd take that as permission. Slowly he leaned forward and touched his lips to hers. Warm. Soft. Compliant. He cradled her face between both hands and trailed light kisses across her forehead. Her temple. Her cheek. Then he caught her mouth again with his.

She melted against him. Responded to him.

Good thing the railing anchored them both, because his legs were no more help holding them up than hers seemed to be.

Keep it light. Keep it light.

Somehow the voice of reason was loud enough to hear above the pounding of his blood. Barely. He pulled back slowly, reluctantly. "You're amazing, Linnea," he whispered. "Never forget it."

"Logan." Her arms wrapped around his neck, and her fingers tangled in his hair. "What are you doing to me?"

"Kissing you." He pressed his lips against one eyelid, then the other. "I don't want to stop."

Linnea trembled in his arms. "Me either." She nestled against his shoulder.

Logan held her tight for a long moment. How had this happened? He'd been determined to treat her like the fragile butterfly she was. He hadn't meant to make any promises he couldn't keep.

Jacob would never have gotten into a situation like this. Jacob had never kissed a woman in his life — at least if one didn't count family members — until Eden, and he'd waited until he could tell her he loved her. Jacob was a better man than Logan.

Linnea stirred against him.

What if she asked a question he wasn't ready to answer? He kissed her again, and she responded with passion that surprised him.

He shouldn't have done this. She was probably hearing wedding bells. Funny thing, he could almost hear them himself, but that was silly. He barely knew her. He shouldn't be kissing someone he barely knew. Logan kissed her again — easier than dealing with questions he couldn't answer. With promises he couldn't make.

Weren't his lips making promises already? Just because it was nonverbal didn't make it any better. With a groan he pushed her away slightly. Enough to get his hands on her arms instead of entangled in an embrace. "Linnea..."

She looked at him, nothing but trust in her pretty blue eyes. "Wow, Logan. That was amazing." She leaned closer again.

No. He couldn't keep doing this. "You're amazing," he whispered. That much at least was true. "We need to take this slower, don't you think?" How much slower? So slow that he'd leave for India before he made promises he couldn't keep?

"Okay."

So simple? Logan groaned. This beautiful woman trusted him far too much. He didn't deserve someone like her. He pushed away from the rail and tucked her against his side. "Let's walk. Show me the rest of the garden."

She slipped her arm around his waist as though they belonged together. He wasn't sure how he'd ever remember the sights of this garden.

Chapter 10

I DON'T THINK YOUR FEET have touched the floor in days." Jasmine sat with her feet curled up under her in the papasan chair in their living room.

Grinning, Linnea wandered over to the window. The bridge stretched, illuminated, across the darkness of the Spokane River. Lights popped on in the houses below the apartment building. "I never knew love could be like this."

Jasmine tucked a bookmark into her paperback and set it on a side table. "Like what?"

"Like Logan. I don't know what I did to deserve him."

"Deserve? I'm not sure anyone deserves love."

Linnea turned from the window. "What do you mean? I know we don't deserve God's love, but that's not what I'm talking about. I'm talking about the love between a woman and a man. Doesn't God want us to be happy?"

Jasmine's eyebrows rose. "People often let us down. God's love is the only one that won't."

Just because her roommate's experience had been bad didn't mean Linnea couldn't be happy. "Logan isn't like that. He's a Christian. He loves God more than anything." How could anyone see Logan at the piano, lost in worship, and doubt?

"I'm just a bit worried about you, that's all."

"Me? You don't need to be. He's a gentleman. He'd never take advantage of me." In fact, Logan held back a little more than Linnea would prefer. Not that she wanted things to go too far, of course, but he rarely let passion speak. Other than through his gorgeous eyes.

"Is he anything like your dad?"

Way to dump a bucket of ice water on her. "Other than they're both members of the male species, no. My dad's full of himself. He just wants to control me and everything in his life." What had Logan said? Dad was a bully.

Jasmine crossed the small living area, poured water into the kettle, and set it on the stove. "Want a cup of tea?"

"Sure. Thanks." Linnea watched her roommate get down two mugs then peruse the cupboard dedicated to foraged herbs. "I thought you'd be happy for me."

"I want to be your friend more than I want to be blindly happy."

What was that supposed to mean? Linnea tipped her head to one side. "Explain."

"I just worry that you're more in love with the idea of being in love than you are in love with Logan. That you were looking for someone to rescue you from your dad, and Logan was the first batter up."

"That's crazy. How can you say that? I moved out of my parents' house before I knew Logan. I mean, we'd met, but I had no idea how important he'd become to me in such a short time."

"Right. You've known him how long now?"

"Well, he and Jacob moved to Bridgeview two months back, but we took on Marietta's garden three weeks ago. That's when it all began."

"Three weeks isn't long enough to really know what someone is like, deep inside." Jasmine's lips pursed.

Linnea braced her hands on the peninsula countertop. "Have you had this conversation with Eden? She and Jacob haven't been dating much longer than we have."

"I don't know Eden as well as I know you. Besides, her circumstances are different."

"It sounds like you regret inviting me to live here. I'll start looking for another place."

Jasmine's hand shot out and touched Linnea's arm. "No, please don't. I'll try to keep my opinions to myself. I'm sorry. It's truly not my intention to hurt you." The kettle whistled, and she busied herself fixing two cups of tea then added a generous dollop of honey to each.

Linnea took a deep breath. She'd probably over-reacted. Again. She sniffed the aromatic liquid. "What's this?"

"Nettle."

Sounded delicious — not. Her roommate knew more about wild herbs than anyone Linnea had ever met. She took a tentative sip. Not Earl Grey, but not bad. They took their cups back to the sitting area, and Linnea curled up in the corner of the couch. Jasmine stared off into nothingness.

"What are you thinking?" As soon as the words escaped, Linnea regretted them. She'd probably get another earful about Logan's perceived shortcomings.

Jasmine shook her head slowly, her gaze focusing on Linnea for a few seconds before drifting away again.

"You told me you'd once been in love. Want to talk about it?"

"Now there's a true case of being in love with being in love." Jasmine's words were barely audible.

Aha. Insight.

"In college, it's all about who you're dating. Did you go to college here?"

Linnea shook her head. "I've just worked for Dad. I don't have a formal education."

"You should get a business degree or something."

Hadn't Logan thought she should start her own landscaping firm? "Maybe. But we were talking about you."

Jasmine grimaced. "For Nathan, it was all about appearances. I thought we were building something for the future, you know? But he wasn't. Oh, he said all the right words, but in the end, it became apparent he'd never meant to stay. And he never asked me to come with him, either. He went from here to UCLA and a new girlfriend in the blink of an eye."

"Ouch."

"Yeah. I was crushed at first. I mean, who wouldn't be? I'd seen our future wrapped up together in a tidy little package with a house in Glenrose and two-point-three kids. Nathan... just didn't want to be alone and bored."

"I'm sorry."

Jasmine shrugged. "I moped for a while, but you know what? I'm better off without him. Anyway, now you know why I'm a bit cynical."

"Logan's not like that."

Jasmine's eyebrows rose above the cup as she sipped.

How could Linnea prove her point? Logan had admitted he liked to travel, that he'd only ever stayed in one place long enough to sock away the funds for his next adventure. That wasn't a life for a married man. For a father. A man like him was just waiting for a woman to make it worth staying in one spot, right? She was that woman for Logan. She knew it. Why else had they met?

"I'm not trying to cast doubts on Logan's love for you." Jasmine met her gaze again. "I'm saying that the choices you face over the next while will affect the rest of your life. Some decisions need to be made with your brain, not your heart. With objectivity, not fuzzy feelings."

"I'll keep that in mind." What else could Linnea say? It wasn't like she'd be able to flip a switch and remove her memory of this evening. But she'd keep reminding herself that her roommate came from a place of hurt that had nothing to do with Logan. Every man was different. Just because Nathan had turned out to be a selfish jerk didn't mean Logan was destined to become one.

Logan pried open the foil packet with a pair of tongs. The baby potatoes he'd picked up at the Kendall Yards Night Market looked and smelled amazing roasted in oil. He'd purchased a bag of ready-made salad and a bottle of dressing from another vendor. Plus the raspberry pie that had called his name. Most residents of Bridgeview supported Hailey and Kass's bakery, but he'd made a pact with himself to stay as far away from Hailey as he could. There were lots of other places to purchase local and tasty options.

That woman didn't seem to catch a hint.

The doorbell rang. Finally. Logan hurried through the house then swept open the front door with a bow. "Welcome, ladies." He pressed a kiss to Linnea's forehead and smiled at Jasmine. "Dinner is nearly ready."

Jasmine looked between him and Linnea. "I could have fended for myself. Really. Just because it was Linnea's night to cook—"

"No, I'm so glad you could come. It seems I've barely had the chance to get to know you." He couldn't tell her he was relieved to have her there, could he? Nope. He'd promised Linnea he could cook and he'd have her over sometime. Then he'd second-guessed the wisdom of that invitation. The addition of her roommate was perfect.

He swept his hand to draw attention to the glass doors at the other end of the living space. "Come on out to the patio, and I'll toss the steaks onto the grill. How do you like yours?"

"Just about walking to my plate." Jasmine grinned.

Linnea shuddered. "No pink in mine, please. And don't make me look at hers."

"Shoe leather, huh?" Logan grabbed the plate of marinated steaks from the fridge before following them. He set one on the burner and adjusted the flame.

"Can I get you a glass of wine? I have a few bottles from Seven Hills in Walla Walla."

"No, thank you." Linnea crossed her long legs. "I'll just have water."

"I'd love a glass, thanks."

On the surface, he and Jasmine were much better suited than he and Linnea, but Jasmine just didn't send sparks through him like Linnea did. Even the fleeting thought made him feel disloyal. He went back into the kitchen, gathered a tray with drinks and everything else he needed, and returned to the patio.

He set water in front of Linnea and wine in front of Jasmine. "How's the massage clinic doing?"

"Pretty well." Jasmine took a sip. "I've been open for about a week now, and some of my clients from North Spokane have followed me over. I think I'll soon be as busy as I want to be."

Logan moved the steak to create cross-hatch marks. "Spoken like a true workaholic."

Jasmine laughed. "Not so much. I only need enough money to support my hobbies. I love foraging and experimenting with what I find."

"She brought home some mushrooms the other day," Linnea put in. "And we didn't even die. They were actually pretty good."

Logan chuckled. "I love fresh mushrooms, but I don't know enough about them to make wise choices."

Jasmine glanced at Linnea. "Maybe next time I find some, we'll have you over."

"Sounds good." Logan added his own steak to the grill. He spread the plates on the table and added salad to each, then opened the foil pack of potatoes and set several on each plate.

"Those smell divine." Linnea leaned closer.

His stomach rumbled. "I hope they taste as good as they smell. I'm starving." A few minutes later he flipped his own steak and added Jasmine's, moving Linnea's to the hot spot on the right. He could only hope a well-done steak would still be tender. He was a medium-rare guy through and through.

"Turn the steak." Jasmine hovered at his elbow.

Already? Well, he didn't have to eat it, so he did as he was told. "Not sure it will even be heated through."

"That's okay. It needs to still say *moo*."

He shook his head, grinning. "Whatever you want. I have to admit that I wouldn't want to eat either of yours." He reached for Linnea's plate and slid her meat onto it then did the same with his. He raised his eyebrows at Jasmine. "Is it ready?"

"I'm sure it is. Thanks."

Logan turned off the grill and plated her steak before sitting down at the table. "Let's pray." He thanked God for friends and good food then gestured for the women to dig in.

"Where did you learn to cook?" Jasmine sliced off a bite of meat.

He shrugged. "A bit here and a bit there. I've been on my own for over ten years." Had it really been that long? Well, yeah. He'd hiked out of his mom's house at sixteen.

Linnea stared at her plate, a pensive expression on her face.

He touched her hand. "Is everything all right?"

She smiled. "I can hardly cook at all. Mom was always too busy to teach me."

"She's doing well, though." Jasmine cut a baby potato in half. "She hasn't poisoned me yet."

Linnea had been so sheltered. Too sheltered. She needed room to grow, but how could he give that to her at this stage? He should've held back. Should've. But now it was too late.

She poked at her salad. "I think I'll take Kass's cooking classes when the community center kitchen is finished. She said something about batch cooking once a month so there are always meal starters in the freezer. And, you know, a plan to follow."

"I remember hearing her talk about it at that community meeting a few weeks ago. She seems very passionate about the concept."

Jasmine nodded. "She is. Plus, she has good ideas. Hailey might be the better baker, but Kass has serious skills on the savory side. She's been making terrific chilled soups this summer. I often pop over at lunchtime and have a bowl."

Linnea shot her roommate a glance.

"I wouldn't know." Logan shifted in his seat. "I stay far away from Hailey. I wouldn't put it past her to ask me out if I set foot in that place."

Jasmine chuckled, but Linnea glanced up quickly then refocused on her plate.

"Hey, don't worry about it." Logan caressed Linnea's hand. "I'd turn her down."

Linnea seemed to have lost her appetite. Somehow he felt like he'd said everything wrong since they got here. What had he done?

Chapter 11

S HE'D EXPECTED THE ENTIRE universe to fill with rainbows and unicorns when she was in love. It didn't, so either she wasn't in love or her expectations had been incorrect. Jasmine's words came to mind. "You're in love with the idea of being in love."

Linnea slammed her spade deep into the topsoil in what would be the community herb garden. Bees and butterflies alike would be drawn to the yarrow, oregano, and feverfew. A long border of chamomile would leave enough for winged things to enjoy as well as plenty of blossoms for tea.

She was like a butterfly.

Ha. She turned the dirt. Had she dreamed everything? If so, she had a better imagination than she'd ever thought. No, Logan's kisses at Manito Park had been real. They'd set her senses on fire. But in the week since then, his kisses hadn't lingered. His eyes no longer seemed to say she filled his world. Last night at his house for dinner, he'd spent more time talking with Jasmine than her.

She was socially inept. She knew that. But he'd known, too, and seemed to love her anyway. Oh, not that he'd ever said that word. She should've read something into that omission sooner. Maybe he just felt sorry for her. Felt he should ask her out because Marietta had pushed them together on this project.

Linnea should have said no. She should have said no to Jasmine, too. She'd still be living at home, contentedly working for her dad. That hadn't been so bad, had it?

Never mind. She'd already felt the urge to spread her wings. To break her way out of her chrysalis and into the fuller life God had for her. She was an adult, for heaven's sake. Hiding in cocoons was for children.

Okay, she wouldn't pressure Logan, not that she had been. Had she? She'd accept whatever he offered and not assume anything he didn't say. She'd guard her heart.

"I didn't know you were working late here tonight."

Linnea jumped at his voice behind her. So much for being guarded. "Hey."

"I texted you, but you didn't answer."

She patted her hip pocket. Just work gloves, no phone. Oh, right. "It was nearly out of juice, so I left it charging at the apartment."

"I was worried."

Linnea pushed out a smile. "No need. What did you want to know?"

"I scored a pair of tickets for the Indians game on Friday night. Want to come?"

Definitely not something she could turn down. "Yes! They're playing Everett, right?"

Logan's laugh reached his eyes. "I should have known you'd have the schedule memorized."

"Duh."

"Hot dogs at the game okay or do you want to get dinner on the way?"

She shook her head. "I don't get off until five, so at the game is fine."

He studied her. "Still working for your dad?"

Her chin rose slightly. "Yes."

"Cool. Do you have another spade? I can give you a hand for a bit before it gets too dark."

Well, that was romantic. She shook her head. "I only have the one. I won't be out here much longer." As it was, the sun had already gone down, but the golden glow down the river lingered.

"Here, let me." Logan reached for the spade. His fingers covered hers.

A tingle shot up her arm. That wouldn't happen if they didn't have chemistry, would it? Was chemistry the same thing as love? Probably not. She released the handle and pulled on her gloves. "I'll work up the clods."

Logan jumped on the spade's shoulders and sank it deep into the ground. "Shouldn't be many of those. Isn't this topsoil?"

"Yes, but it's been exposed to the elements over the winter." She dropped to her knees and broke apart a clump.

"Jacob will be back from Africa on Saturday."

So much for hoping they could talk about whatever was going on between them. "You've missed him?"

He shrugged. "Kind of. It's been weird with him away for a month. I usually travel at least as much as he does."

She glanced up at Logan, but his face was hidden in the shadows. "He travels on the job, right? Is it like a mission or something?"

"Global Sunbeams is a business with a charity arm. Not a mission as such."

"But you work for a housing contractor." She didn't even know which one.

"Yeah. For now. It's not my dream-come-true job."

The beginning of the end. It had been too good to last, but she'd hang onto whatever crumbs he tossed her before he left, as pitiful as that was. Although tickets to a ballgame weren't pathetic. "So if you could do any job, what would it be?"

He shoved the spade into the dirt. "It all requires an education I don't have."

"Guess that makes two of us."

"I've made the choice a dozen times. Save for a semester of college or take a trip overseas. Seeing the world won every time."

Linnea squelched the jealousy. "And travel isn't educational?"

He chuckled and dug in again. "Oh, it is. You just can't get a diploma or take it to the bank."

"You're not too old to do it, you know." At least that's what people kept telling her. Logan was a couple of years older, but not enough to matter. Her mom's friend had gone back to school and started a new career as a hairdresser after her kids left home.

He shrugged. "I suppose. I'm not sure what I'd take, though."

She studied him in the shadows. "You're itching to go again, aren't you?"

Logan leaned on the handle and looked down at her. "It might always be a part of me. Don't worry, though. I won't bail in the middle of this project."

Her gut soured. No hint of anything longer term? How to confirm her fears. She should've been nicer to Alex.

"Hey, look, there's Adriana."

Logan followed the direction Linnea pointed to spot a single mom from their neighborhood shepherding her eight-year-old son down the stadium aisle toward them. Sam jittered with excitement.

Had Logan ever been so giddy about anything at Sam's age? He couldn't remember.

"Adriana!" Linnea leaned and waved.

Adriana glanced up as she and Sam edged into the row in front of them. Her face blossomed into a smile as she waved back. "Hey, guys. Date night?"

Logan wrapped his fingers around Linnea's. "Sure is. Looks like the same for you."

Sam had barely glanced their direction. He was focused on the diamond below.

"He's sports obsessed." Adriana shook her head. "I try to bring him to at least one game a month, whatever is in season."

"That's great. Wish my mom had done the same."

A quick flash of sympathy zipped across Adriana's face. "You grew up without a dad, too?" Her hand rested on Sam's shoulder. "It's rough on a little boy. Tough for his sister, too, mind you."

Logan had met Adriana's younger child, a precocious girl of about seven. Someone who pushed all the buttons all the time. "Yeah, my dad bailed when I was a baby."

"I'm sorry. Stefan didn't leave us on purpose. He was a firefighter and died a hero."

"I remember hearing about it on the news a few years ago." Linnea disengaged her fingers from his. "I'm so sorry."

"Thanks. It's been four years. We still have our moments, but we've mostly adjusted."

"A person does," Logan said.

Sam tugged at Adriana's arm, pointing at the players warming up. She conferred with him a moment before turning back to them.

"Listen, I've been meaning to ask you guys something." She looked between him and Linnea.

"Oh, what's that?"

"I'm having a dinner party next Sunday night. Not day after tomorrow, but next week. Would you two like to come? I've invited Francesca and Tad and Rebekah and Wade so far."

Logan glanced at Linnea as he wrapped his fingers around hers. Again. "Want to, babe?"

"I, um..."

"It's just going to be a relaxing evening to get to know our neighbors a bit better. I'd thought to invite Jacob and Eden, too, but he's still in Africa, right?"

"He'll be home tomorrow."

Adriana's face brightened. "Oh, I'll hold seats for them, too, then. I'll get in touch with Eden and confirm." She glanced at Linnea. "Or did you have other plans already?"

"No other plans." Linnea tugged her hand out of Logan's as she smiled at Adriana. "That sounds fun. What can I bring?"

"Nothing at all but your appetites. It's casual, out on the deck. We have a great view of the river out back. I'm so glad you're coming."

"Mom!" Sam yanked at Adriana's arm. "The game's starting."

Adriana grinned at Logan and Linnea then bent to give Sam her full attention.

Logan glanced at the woman beside him, but she was as focused on the diamond as the boy in front of them. If Logan hadn't previously been to a ballgame with her, he'd suspect her of ignoring him. Now, he wasn't sure. But the fact that she'd pulled away from him twice definitely meant something.

Logan was the perfect gentleman, even though she'd snubbed him several times during the game. He kept reaching for her hand, but she couldn't handle the contact. Not when everything in her screamed to throw her arms around him and kiss him. But he'd been so aloof all week, and now, in public, he wanted to be touchy-feely? Called her babe?

He slid into the driver's seat and glanced across at her in the dusk. "Did you have a good time?"

Loaded question. "Too bad Spokane lost, but it looked like Sam had fun, regardless."

"How about you?"

Yeah, she hadn't thought he'd let that go. Was she brave enough to reply honestly? She pictured a butterfly struggling out of its chrysalis. There was pain in gaining freedom. Otherwise, she was allowing the silken strands to harden around her again. "Mixed," she said at last.

His hand, which had been reaching for the ignition switch, stopped in mid-air and slowly settled to his thigh. "How's that?"

"The game was good, other than of course I wish we'd won."

"Uh huuuh." Logan waited.

Here went nothing. "I have to admit to being a bit confused, though. I'm not sure where I stand with you." She could feel his eyes on her, but no way was she meeting them. She stared out the windshield, watching cars around them head out of the parking lot toward Havana Street.

"I'm not sure where I stand with you, either." His voice was low.

She probably deserved that.

"Linnea, I..."

She waited.

"I never expected this."

Her eyebrows went up of their own accord and she couldn't resist a peek at him. He stared at his hands clenched on his thighs. "Define *this*," she said at last.

"You. Me. I never expected to have... feelings."

"Me, neither." Okay, that was a lie. She'd been attracted to him from the first time she'd heard him play piano at church. She'd never expected him to look twice at her. Not when there were so many other single young women who were prettier and more articulate. Hailey. Kass. Jasmine. Others. He'd never have noticed her if Marietta hadn't thrown them together. Now he felt a sense of obligation. Those were the feelings he was talking about, for sure.

"I like you a lot, Linnea."

She waited for the other shoe to drop.

"But I'm not sure I've got what it takes to make you happy."

Linnea crossed her arms over her chest. "And what do you think that will be?"

"You need someone who will be here for the long haul. Someone with a steady job who doesn't have itchy feet."

"Oh, you mean someone like Alex Santoro?"

He flinched.

Good. "I don't love Alex, Logan. He's a friend. Nothing more."

"But—"

"You're still doing it, you know."

That got his attention. "Doing what?"

"Assuming you know what I want. What will make me happy. You're still trying to protect me."

He glanced her way. "I guess so. I'm sorry."

Did he really mean those words? "Logan, do you want to know what I'd like?"

He searched her face but didn't reply.

"I'll tell you. I want a better relationship with God. I want a job out from under my dad's thumb. A career." Huh. Now that she'd said it out loud, she realized she meant it. "I want a husband who loves me and listens to me without smothering me. I want kids. I want to see the world. I want a lot of things, Logan Dermott. I'm not expecting one man to hand me my heart's desire on a silver platter. That's not his job."

"Linnea, I..."

This time when he reached for her hand, she met him halfway.

His callused thumb rubbed over her tender palm. "Will you give me another chance? I want to see you become that woman."

The chrysalis weakened just a little as her cramped wings fluttered against the bonds. "I don't want any promises you can't keep."

Logan hesitated then nodded. "Here's something I know is true. I want to get to know you better. I like you, Linnea. I like you a lot."

She noticed he didn't say love, but this was better. She wouldn't have believed the other word.

Chapter 12

FRANCESCA PLAYED FOR CHURCH that Sunday morning, giving Logan the opportunity to sit beside Linnea toward the back during the service. She shifted away when he touched her, not enough to be a big deal, but enough that he noticed.

He watched with envy as Jacob and Eden, closer to the front, held hands during the singing and snuck smiling glances at each other. A month apart didn't seem to have hurt their relationship one speck. Logan knew with certainty that if he left for a month, whatever he had with Linnea would be burned toast. Unlike his housemate, Logan's job wouldn't send him further away than Spokane Valley, so he wouldn't have a good excuse.

The old restlessness stirred in his gut but, for the first time, it was mixed with a different kind of longing. How could a guy want to leave and stay at the same time? This was crazy. He'd thought to protect Linnea. Now it seemed she was holding her own, and he was the one in danger of falling past the point of no return.

He had no clue what Pastor Tomas preached about, but when the benediction had been said, he leaned closer to Linnea, brushing his sleeve against her arm. "I'd like to get some take-out and spend the afternoon in Marietta's garden with you. What do you say?"

She regarded him thoughtfully. "Mexican, and you're on."

More relief flooded him than he'd thought possible. "I don't want to dig and plant today. I just want to get to know you better. Talk."

"Okay." Linnea glanced around the thinning crowd. "I need a real day off, anyway. I think we're on point to get the garden finished before the snow flies."

"When's that?"

She met his gaze and smiled. "It varies, of course. Some years we have none before Christmas. Other times, we get a snowfall in October."

"A moving target, then."

"You could say that."

Logan stood and tugged Linnea up beside him, not letting go. "Come on. I drove today, so let's go get lunch."

"I should change."

He let his gaze linger on her slender body, clad in a lacy tank and gray capris. Her long hair, done in a French braid, swung nearly to her waist. "No need. I have a picnic blanket in the trunk we can sit on."

"Okay."

For some reason, she was giving him a second chance. He'd take it... and try not to mess things up again.

111

Linnea leaned back against the sycamore in the garden. Not far away, Logan stretched out on the grass, staring up at the leafy branches.

"Thanks for lunch. That was a great burrito."

"You're welcome. The other night you said you wanted a real career. What did you mean?"

Okay, he'd meant it when he said they needed to get to know each other better. She waved a hand around the community garden. "I want to learn how to do this properly. My dad is content to do mostly lawn maintenance, but I'd really like to design gardens. Do more with permaculture, for instance. Rebekah and Wade dropped by the other day to discuss their food forest project with Jasmine. It all sounds so cool."

"So you've given more thought to food security like we talked about."

She plucked a tall stem of grass and began rolling it tightly. "Yes, I have. Hard not to, rooming with Jasmine. She's really into foraging. Anything to do with food, really."

"Is there a college in Spokane where you can study landscaping?"

"The community college." Linnea eyed him. "But I'm thinking about Edmonds over near Seattle. They have a two-year horticulture program."

Logan pulled to sitting and wrapped both arms around his knees. "Really?"

"I'd need to save up money. So maybe a year from now." What would he hear from that about their relationship? She wouldn't have to apply for a few more months. But he'd already said he wanted to travel again soon.

"You're serious."

"Yeah, I am. I'm twenty-four, Logan. I missed my chance to get a degree or even a diploma any younger, and I can't think of a thing to be gained by waiting longer. Not if I want to build my own life." She heard the double meaning in her words. If he upped his game, she might give him another chance. But now that she'd considered the rest of her life, she couldn't simply *un*consider it.

Logan might be in it, or he might not. Either way, she didn't want to mow the Ridleys' lawn forever. The butterfly wings pushed against the chrysalis, weakening it. She needed to fly free.

"It wasn't so long ago that you seemed to need protecting. What happened?"

She glanced at him, but the expression on his face seemed sincere. Confused, even. "I grew up a bit, I guess." Should she tell him more? Might as well go for broke. "Jasmine accused me of being in love with the idea of being in love. She wasn't far wrong. Before I accepted Marietta's project, I hadn't really done anything on my own. Just worked for Dad and behaved myself like a good little girl. This garden upset the cart."

Logan's eyes focused on hers. "What made you take this on without your father's blessing?"

That telltale flush rose in her cheeks. "You."

He chuckled, but choked it off as suddenly as it started. "You're serious."

Linnea nodded. "When I stopped by to meet Marietta, I was intrigued but rather intimidated. She's... an interesting person. I was halfway to saying no."

"But then..."

She clenched her hands together. "But then she said she'd asked you to do the carpentry parts and, before I knew it, you were there. Flirting with me."

Logan grimaced. "Sorry."

"For flirting?"

"For making you uncomfortable."

"I didn't believe it was real, but I wanted to pretend it was."

"You did?" He glanced at her then away.

"I thought you were pretty hot." Just like her cheeks at the moment. She closed her eyes. What could be worse than seeing him laugh at her confession? He'd already started to.

His hand covered hers. "Linnea."

Didn't sound like laughter. She peered at him through lowered lashes.

He looked serious. Contrite. "I don't deserve you. I wish I did."

"I'm not sure what you mean by that."

"I felt sorry for you at first."

Linnea pulled her hands free. This was getting to be a pattern.

"Let me finish. Please."

"Okay." Her word was little above a whisper.

"But you've proven me so wrong. You're far stronger than I gave you credit for. You're leaving me in the dust."

"It's not so different."

"But it is. You've taken a hard look at your life and figured out what changes you need to make."

"What's stopping you from doing the same?" Linnea felt her eyes widen as her hand clapped over her mouth. "I'm sorry. I shouldn't have said that."

Logan stretched out onto the blanket as though she'd flattened him. "No, it's a valid question. One I wish I had the answer to, but I don't." He held her gaze. "Not at the moment, anyway."

A shrill whistle came from over by the sidewalk. Linnea tore her eyes from Logan's and glanced over. "It's Eden and Jacob." What a time to be interrupted by the lovebirds. Only Jasmine — and now Logan — knew anything about her misgivings. Her thought process. She wasn't going to dump that on anyone else, especially someone she barely knew.

Logan sat up. "Hey, man! Get over here. Let us show you around."

Was that relief in his voice? Relief they'd been interrupted? She'd follow his lead in the conversation.

Jacob and Eden sauntered closer, hand in hand, taking in the sight of the half-formed lot. "It's looking good," said Jacob.

Linnea stood. "It *will* look good." This stage, between the pretty plans and the finished garden, seemed to drag forever. Or maybe it was because of the flux in their relationship that made it feel interminable. Maybe things would get better now that they'd cleared the air. If that's what they'd done.

Now, how to keep Logan's housemate and his girlfriend from suspecting that everything wasn't a bed of roses? Because listening to the two guys joke right now made her think Logan hadn't told Jacob anything about it.

"Okay, out with it." Jacob dropped into his favorite arm-chair in their shared living room.

Logan draped the headphones around his neck and turned down the volume on the keyboard. "Out with what?"

"What's going on with you and Linnea?"

"Already told you. We're dating. Have been since about the time you left for Africa."

"And how's it going?"

Logan switched to another, peppier, worship song. "Fine."

"Give it up, Dermott. There's something going on beneath the surface. If I just listened to your words, I'd think you were all coochie-coo. But both of your body language said something different."

After they'd hung out at Marietta's garden for a while, Eden had invited them to her house for supper. Logan had gotten back from walking Linnea home minutes before Jacob strolled in the front door.

"Every relationship has hiccups, dude. Explain to me how you're getting along with Eden's goat."

Jacob's face flushed. "We're not talking about me. We're talking about you."

"I guess we're not talking about the same thing then."

"Look, I'm asking because I care about you. You're my best friend. My buddy."

"It's just a bit of growing pains, okay? Linnea's changed since I first met her. Moved in with Jasmine. Begun thinking about the future."

Jacob's eyes gleamed.

"Not what you think." Logan's fingers sped up on the keyboard. "She's talking about going away to college for two years."

"So that's not a biggie, right? You've been saving money for India."

"Yeah." Even he could tell there wasn't much enthusiasm behind his voice.

"Having second thoughts?"

Logan shrugged and bent over the keyboard. If his housemate only knew he was having second thoughts about almost everything in his life. "It'll work out."

"What will? Linnea? Or India?"

"Either. Both."

"Dermott."

He sighed. "What, Riehl?"

"Why don't you pray about it, decide what you want, and go after it with everything you've got?"

The praying part had been drifting away the past couple of weeks. "Yeah."

"Because that's the only way you're going to find God's will. It doesn't wander over to someone who's not looking for it."

Logan swiveled on the keyboard bench. "Now you're an expert?"

His housemate had the grace to flush. "Not an expert, exactly."

"Well, I'm glad to hear you say that, because things don't look that rosy with you and Eden, either."

"What makes you say that?"

"Oh, don't sound so defensive. I'm not blind, deaf, or stupid. You two are walking on eggshells still. Have you really truly talked about her goat?"

Jacob's eyes narrowed. "I petted Pansy today."

"And I bet you did it enthusiastically."

"Hey."

"Don't go poking at my relationship with Linnea if you don't want scrutiny on yours with Eden." He swung around and began to play again. What song matched his mood? He couldn't think of anything.

"Eden and I are going to look at the properties over at Kendall Yards next weekend, thanks to Linnea's suggestion. They're not zoned for goats there."

If Jacob couldn't see the crash in their relationship coming, there was nothing Logan could say to make a difference. His housemate lived in his own little world.

"Linnea likes goats." Logan couldn't resist the dig. "She told me she wants to get on the list for some of Pansy's milk."

Jacob snorted.

"Rather undignified sound there."

"It's just a goat."

"For your information, Riehl, that goat is a much bigger deal between you and Eden than anything that's between me and Linnea. So she wants to go to college. Why not? A diploma in horticulture will open all kinds of doors for her."

"And you're going to sit around and wait two years for her?"

Logan bit his lip. "Maybe."

"I'll believe it when I see it. You don't look that kind of in love to me."

"Maa."

Jacob surged to his feet. "What was that for?"

"The goat, dude. If anyone isn't focusing on the future with both eyes peeled, it's you. I at least am facing the options in front of me."

Jacob opened his mouth and closed it again. He swerved into the kitchen. "Want a glass of iced tea?"

Classic Jacob evasion. "Sure. Thanks." Logan followed his friend into the other room. "Look, I'm sorry. I know you're all out of whack from traveling halfway around the world. It's not fair of me to pick on you before you're caught up with this time zone again."

Jacob set two glasses on the counter and filled them. "I'm trying to remember it's only because you care."

"Yeah, it is."

"Goes both ways, Dermott. Goes both ways."

Chapter 13

"How's Nonna's garden coming along?" Francesca sipped a glass of mead on Adriana's back deck a week later.

"Pretty well." Linnea didn't dare glance at Logan. "The beds are all in place, and we'll get another truckload of topsoil later in the fall. I've been transplanting some herbs and perennials, but a lot of that will come when the weather cools off more."

"Nights are definitely cooler now than a few weeks ago. Thank the Lord," put in Rebekah.

She must be due to pop that baby out nearly any time. Linnea could only imagine how summer heat must feel to someone so unwieldy.

"I built a potting shed yesterday." Logan lifted his wine glass in salute.

See? Another way they were different. Linnea couldn't even pretend to enjoy the acrid taste. Tonight she'd opted for ice water and made sure Rebekah kept well supplied, too.

"Nice," said Francesca's husband, Tad. "So you're on track to finish this fall?"

"Sure are."

If Logan's nonchalance was anything to go by, things were just fine between him and Linnea. The urge to rock the boat nearly overcame her. How could he keep pretending like this?

"It's such an exciting time to live in Bridgeview." Francesca turned to Wade and Rebekah. "The garden, the community center, the food forest you guys are putting in."

The young couple had been instrumental in getting grants to plant fruit and nut trees on a city-owned lot on the riverfront, as well as other perennial food crops. Permaculture. One of these days Linnea needed to pick their brains more about that topic.

"We're even thinking about getting a few chickens ourselves," Francesca went on.

Linnea laughed. "That must be Jasmine's idea."

"It is." Francesca grinned. "Easy for her to say, living in an apartment, right? But still, we might do it. It would be good for Tieri and Luca to grow up understanding where food comes from."

"We plan on a few chickens next summer, too." Wade slid his arm around his wife and patted her huge belly with his other hand. "Seemed like we had enough to deal with this year without adding that to the mix."

No wonder Linnea felt like the odd person out. Two married couples, one with children and one who would have their first any day now. Trying to imagine her and Logan really being part of this group was beyond her skill set. If only Eden and Jacob were out on the deck, too, but they were helping Adriana in the kitchen.

Talk dwindled. Past the deck and a shade-loving flower garden, Adriana's chickens scratched around inside their large pen. The river gurgled past not far beyond. A few birds swooped through, and the buzz of a honeybee or two murmured through the air. What a beautiful property.

Linnea inhaled slowly, feeling peace enter along with air.

Logan's fingers twined around hers and she stiffened slightly. He hadn't stopped pretending that everything was okay, that nothing had really changed between them. As soon as she could do so without seeming obvious, she pulled her hand away and reached for her water glass without glancing over.

What was she going to do about him? Why couldn't she believe there was no unruly current beneath the placid surface of their relationship? He was all about holding her hand in public, but hadn't kissed her in over a week. Not even a peck on the cheek or forehead. How was she supposed to figure out what he wanted?

Tad turned toward Logan. "You still playing three-on-three with the guys?"

"Not much. The garden has been keeping me pretty busy, and they rarely need an extra player."

Tad laughed. "I can't keep up with them. Peter, Basil, and Alex have been playing together since they were kids."

Linnea hadn't seen Jasmine's older brother Basil around much lately. Alex, on the other hand...

Maybe she should reconsider Alex. He was a good guy with a degree in accounting. How much steadier could a man be? Maybe it was better to have someone dependable around than one who made her veins smolder and freeze in turn.

How much more could she handle of Logan's hot and cold? She couldn't imagine being this frustrated with Alex. This desperate for a kiss and a commitment. But watching Francesca and Tad... maybe that level of passion didn't stick around, anyway. They'd been married, what, six or seven years, maybe? They looked comfortable, not like a couple who couldn't wait to get alone to get their hands on each other. So if the passion didn't last, what did it matter if it was there to start with? Wouldn't it be better to start with mutual respect than a racing heart?

She respected Alex. Yeah, he'd risen to Logan's baiting. It would have taken a saint not to. But other than that, he was good. Jasmine liked her little brother and was proud of him for landing a job at one of the most prestigious firms in Spokane. Marietta boasted of him same as her other grandchildren.

Would her father like Alex better than Logan?

Where had that thought even come from? Dad wasn't wired to appreciate any man who sniffed around his little girl. Alex was no more likely to win that round than Logan, although his shorter hair might help.

She shook her head.

"You okay, babe?" asked Logan in a low voice.

Guilty. She blinked and focused on his blue eyes, filled with concern. "Fine, thanks."

Eden poked her head around the French door from the dining room. "We're about to bring out dinner, if everyone would like to find your seat at the table. Violet made place cards for you."

Before Linnea could rise, Logan was up and reaching for her hand. The perfect gentleman when he wanted to be. He rested his hand on the small of her back and guided her toward the long table further down the deck. Her name, printed by a childish hand, was accompanied by a purple flower. Next to her place sat a card for Logan with a strawberry colored on it.

Logan held her chair and seated her before taking the chair to her left.

"Thank you." She smiled at him. Her mouth dried as she caught the undercurrent in his blue eyes.

He didn't mean anything by it. It was just his way with women. She knew that.

Alex would definitely be a safer choice.

Logan reached for Linnea's hand as they left Adriana's, but she seemed focused on adjusting her purse strap. Fifty thousand evasions tonight was one too many. He glanced over his shoulder. Jacob, Eden, Wade, and Rebekah were already half a block away as they strolled the other direction, chatting and laughing. Francesca and Tad lingered on Adriana's front steps, caught in the porch light.

No one was paying any attention to him and Linnea. He shifted closer. "Want to talk about it?"

"Talk about what?"

"Whatever is bugging you."

"Nothing's changed, Logan."

"No, you're right. I thought we'd cleared the air the other day, but I'm just as perplexed now as I was then."

She took a deep breath and shoved both her hands into the pockets of her capris. "You think you're confused? Try being in my shoes."

Well, at least she was talking. "Tell me."

"You honestly don't know?"

This was classic girl talk. The kind where a guy was supposed to fish answers from thin air and get them right the first time. "I'm a member of the male species. Can you clarify the situation for me?"

She stopped in the middle of the sidewalk. "You're kidding me."

He waited a few feet away. If he thought she'd let him, he'd close the gap and kiss her. Even the thought surprised him. His gut churned. How could she do this to him? Make him sweat for weeks, not knowing whether they were okay or not?

"What is going on in your head, Logan Dermott? You tell me you like me, but the only time you come anywhere near me is when we're around a bunch of people, and then you want to hold my hand like nothing's wrong. What, so no one will suspect we're not okay? So Hailey won't hear that you're really not as taken as she thinks you are?"

Ouch. "What's Hailey got to do with anything?"

"I don't know! You tell me."

He shook his head. "Are you jealous of Hailey? Because I don't even like her. I never have. I can't think why you'd get the impression she means anything to me."

"You're doing it again."

Frustration boiled over the top. "Doing what again?" He grasped her by both shoulders. "What do you want from me?"

Linnea stood stock still under his hands. She stared straight into his eyes from mere inches away and sucked in her lips.

He wanted nothing more than to kiss her like he'd dreamed of doing again since that day in the Japanese garden. The newer, bolder Linnea probably slap him if he did. It might be worth it. Then again, it might not. The garden wasn't finished, and they had to work together for at least a few more weeks. He dropped his hands.

Her gaze hardened. "And you think *you're* confused?" Linnea demanded.

How could she even ask that? Couldn't she read anything on his face? Couldn't she feel the tension between them?

"Very," he ground out.

"Well, that makes two of us." She pushed past him on the sidewalk and strode away.

Logan hurried to catch up. "Linnea. Wait."

She stopped so suddenly he nearly ran her over and whirled, her hair whipping out and flicking his face.

Wait. Were there tears glistening on her cheeks? He reached out and brushed one away with his thumb.

She flinched. "Logan, don't do this to me."

No wonder guys went on those he-man expeditions in the wilderness and howled at the moon. He was only two breaths away from doing it here and now. Only there was no moon, and the coyotes were already lamenting its absence from down along the river bottom. Seriously, was any woman worth what Linnea had put him through? How could she blame him for all of it? It was a two-way street and, to his way of thinking, he was getting the rough end of the deal.

"You want to know what I want?" His words came out rough and angry.

"What?"

"This." He reached for her before she could step away, pulled her tightly against his chest, and covered her mouth with his. He poured all his frustration and passion into that kiss. For the first second or two, her lips were flaccid beneath his. He'd shocked her, no doubt. But then her arms came around his waist and she responded taste for taste.

Logan groaned and deepened the kiss, his hands roving her back, clutching her close.

Suddenly she jerked out of his arms, no doubt leaving his mouth puckered like a guppy. "What are you doing?"

"Kissing you. Much like you were kissing me." Already his body chilled where her touch was gone. "I'd kind of like to do that again."

"Use your words."

"Huh?" Sounded like the kissing was off again.

"Why did you kiss me?"

"Because I l-l-like you a lot." She was probably looking for the *love* word, but could he honestly say that? Could he lay his soul bare for her to stomp on, as infuriating as she'd been the past week or two? Not until he was sure.

"Do you *like* me a lot when you're ignoring me, or only when you want something?"

"What are you talking about?"

"You are infuriating." She bit off every syllable. "Logan Dermott, I don't know what you're thinking, but I can't live like this. I can't date a man who can't talk to me about his feelings. Who can't decide whether he's cold or hot. I can't do it. Don't make me try."

Wait a minute. Was she breaking up with him after a kiss as potent as the one they'd just shared? *Because* of it? That made no sense. If the kiss didn't show her how much he cared about her, what could mere words say?

And she said *he* was infuriating. "Lin—"

Her hand sliced down between them. "I'll try to stay out of your way at the garden. Hand your receipts in to Ray when you're done."

"Babe—"

"Don't, Logan. Don't even start." She turned on her heel and strode up the street, her lithe form swaying slightly.

What had happened to the fragile butterfly he'd met not two months before? He should be glad she didn't need a protector. Why had he thought he'd done her any favors? All that had gotten him was a stomped-on heart.

Was it possible he was actually in love with Linnea Ranta, and she'd walked out of his life?

Chapter 14

WHY HADN'T LOGAN PHONED? Texted? Stopped by the garden when she was there? That he hadn't contacted her for an entire week was proof enough that he didn't love her. Didn't care. If a man was really dense enough not to figure out what he'd done wrong — and she'd spelled it out to him — then he wasn't the one for her.

Dread churned deep in her gut. Dread that she'd driven him away. But no. When she pulled out the events of the past few weeks and re-examined them, she hadn't made a mistake. He really had been hot and cold but mostly lukewarm. Love wasn't lukewarm. He was nothing more than a flirt, and she'd fallen for it. What she'd fallen into, she could climb out of, given time.

She mowed and clipped and weeded other people's yards all week. If she owned this space or that one, how would she want it to look? What changes would she make? The game distracted her from Logan for entire minutes at a time. Moving out of Spokane and going to college would be a good thing. How would she save up any money on the meager salary Dad paid her? Maybe she could get a second job in the pre-Christmas rush as a waitress or a clerk in the evenings. If she wanted to make a change, she was going to have to get proactive.

Linnea parked the Ranta Landscaping truck beside the apartment and swung out, weary to the bone. She clomped up the two flights of stairs and into the space she shared with Jasmine. First, a shower to sluice off the dirt and grass clippings. Then she'd start supper. She was pretty sure she had a plan. Maybe hot water would help her remember what it was.

She stepped out of the bathroom a few minutes later in clean jeans and a T-shirt, still-damp hair braided from her forehead back.

"Hey, Linnea. Long day at work?"

She blinked Alex into focus where he sat on the far end of the sofa. Jasmine waved from her papasan chair. Had they been there when Linnea stumbled through? Good thing she hadn't wrapped her dripping body in a towel and dashed to her room.

"Um, yeah. You could say so."

Alex had loosened his necktie under the open collar of a light-blue button-down shirt. Black dress pants, crisply creased, ended in black leather shoes. His dark wavy hair just brushed his collar.

Alex. Logan. How much more different could two men be? Logan's hair was too long and always slightly — or a lot — messy. Linnea would bet he didn't even own dress pants or a tie.

She found a smile for Alex. "You staying for supper? It's my night to cook."

The siblings exchanged glances.

"I could, but may I get dinner ordered in? I'm in the mood to celebrate."

Her cooking would never be cause for celebration. "Oh? What are we celebrating?"

Alex grinned, the dimple in his left cheek deepening. Logan's dimple was on the right. *Good grief. Stop thinking about Logan.*

"I got a promotion and a raise today."

"Congratulations! That's great." Linnea perched on the arm at the other end of the sofa. "They must be happy with your work."

Alex turned toward her, curling one knee onto the sofa. His eyes gleamed with excitement. "I'm still a couple of promotions away from a corner office, but I'm young. I've got time."

Logan's big dream was to earn enough money to travel for a few months. Alex was going places right here in Spokane. How had she ever thought Logan was the better man?

"That's really great, Alex. Thanks for inviting Jasmine and me to be part of your celebration." She glanced at her roommate. "Sounds way better than whatever I was going to cook."

Alex laughed. "You didn't even ask where I was ordering in from."

"You didn't even ask what was on the menu here."

"Touché. Indian sound good?"

"Mmm. Butter chicken and naan. You're on."

"And that lamb korma." Jasmine moaned. "I need to learn to cook Indian."

Who needed to spend months' worth of earnings to go to a foreign land when the food was available right here?

Alex pulled out his smart phone and placed the order.

Jasmine unfolded from the papasan. "If I have half an hour, I'd like to hit the shower before dinner arrives. You two talk nicely to each other while I'm out of the room."

When the sound of the shower started, Linnea risked a glance at Alex.

He was watching her. "Still going out with Dermott?"

Heat rose in her cheeks. "Not really."

"Oh?" Hope rose in the single word.

"We're still finishing up the project for your grandmother, but we don't run into each other much. We're both pretty busy."

"Linnea, I can get tickets for the symphony next weekend. Would you like to go?"

Hadn't she been trying to convince herself for a week or more that she was over Logan and that Alex would suit her much better? She'd never dreamed the opportunity to test her theory would come so quickly. "Um, that sounds great."

"Really? You'll come with me?"

She dared to meet his intense gaze. "I'd love to." It might not be a ballgame, but a concert was a good choice for a first date.

"It's Saturday at eight. May I take you for dinner before the show?"

Definitely full-on first date material. She should be feeling a flutter of excitement round about now. It seemed more like a slippery slope, but that was silly. She'd known Alex since high school. He was a good guy. Safe. Best of all, he wasn't Logan.

Logan turned off the table saw in Ray Santoro's shop and stacked the trimmed board with the others the same length.

"You're working late tonight." His host leaned against the doorjamb, silhouetted against the glow from the street lamp.

What time was it, anyway? "I'm sorry. I didn't think I'd bother anyone out here."

"No problem. It's only ten-thirty. I just got in from work and heard the saw. Has my mother spoken to you about the permaculture workshop?"

Logan stared at him blankly. "No. What workshop is that?" He hadn't seen Marietta in a while. He'd been avoiding the garden any hours Linnea might be there, which seemed to eliminate talking to Marietta as well. Suited him just fine.

Ray shook his head. "I told her to talk to you first, but no. Mamma always acts impulsively."

Patience.

"It's a full day workshop at Green Acres Farm in Idaho. Up near Galena Landing."

Logan's heart beat faster. "I know where that is. I've got friends there."

Ray grinned. "Well, that's good, then. Mamma paid for spots for you and Linnea. It's the first Saturday in October. Starts at eight in the morning."

Two weeks away. "Have you mentioned it to Linnea?" Because there was a distinct chance she'd refuse to go, even though the workshop sounded right up her alley.

"No, not yet. I'm sure you see her oftener than I do." Ray winked. "I'll let you discuss it with her and get back to me."

Logan let out a long breath. "I haven't seen much of her lately."

"Oh?" Ray glanced out the doorway toward the community garden, though of course it was too dark to see a thing. "Progress has been made, though."

"I kind of... blew it. Not sure how." A week of being unable to get her words out of his head had given him some clues, though. She was tougher than he'd given her credit for.

Sympathy gleamed in the older man's eyes. "Do you want to talk about it?"

Logan hesitated a moment. He really had no one to give him counsel. Jacob had apparently gotten over Eden's goat and was floating around somewhere in the clouds with a beatific beam on his face. The guy was of no earthly good. Even when his feet had been planted on solid ground, his advice was suspect.

Ray Santoro, on the other hand, was the father of five twenty-somethings, four of them sons. One of them Alex. If Ray wasn't going to remind him of that, Logan wouldn't bring it up. "Yeah. Maybe."

The older man nodded. "Let me go in and change. I'll grab a bottle of wine and we can sit out on the patio. I'm sure Grace has already gone to bed, and Evan is likely out with friends."

"I don't mean to keep you up."

Ray waved a hand. "It takes me a while to unwind after work anyway. Don't worry about it. I'll be right back." His footsteps faded.

Logan swept the sawdust off the shop floor and straightened the tools. This was crazy. He should just head down the hill and apologize to Ray for standing him up later. But God knew, he had no father figure in his life. How pathetic was it that he'd confide in his rival's dad?

But Alex wasn't his rival. Not really. They didn't live in caveman days when two Neanderthals clubbed each other and the winner dragged the prize off to his cave. No, Linnea had a choice.

A bottle thunked onto the patio table, followed by two clinking glasses. Logan flipped off the light and closed the shop door behind him. A row of solar lights led the way to the patio where Ray stretched out in a reclining deck chair. "Help yourself, son."

Logan's heart softened just a little. He poured a glass, unable to read the label in the dark. He settled into a cushioned chair near Ray.

The older man sipped his wine. "Tell me about your growing up years. What was your father like?"

And that's where it all started, right? "My parents never married. I don't know my dad real well. He left when I was little more than a baby." No wonder he didn't know how to do relationships. Had he ever observed a good one?

"So you are an only child?"

"No. I have two younger sisters. My mother didn't marry their fathers, either."

"It is a broken world."

Logan nodded. That about summed it up.

"And yet you have found the One who has promised to be a Father to the fatherless. I have heard you play the piano, son. You play as one who worships your heavenly Father. You have a great gift."

"Thank you. Music... sometimes I feel it is all I truly have."

"So what brought you to Spokane?"

"Jacob and I have been friends for a few years, and he got a position with Global Sunbeams. He didn't know anyone here so I tagged along. It was pretty easy to find a job in construction. Spokane is as good a city as any I've lived." Better than many. Staying permanently had never even crossed his mind anyplace else he'd wandered through.

"It is a good place, and Bridgeview is the best neighborhood." Ray chuckled. "I may be biased. I grew up here and have never been away for long."

"I can't even imagine." But he wanted to. The call of the Taj Mahal was barely a faint whisper, but was there any point in staying here to watch Linnea mother the next generation of Santoros?

"Tell me about Linnea."

"She's pretty amazing."

Ray chuckled and lifted his wine glass.

Logan had all but forgotten his. He took a sip. "No, she is. Really. She has no formal training in landscape architecture, but you've seen how perfectly the garden is turning out. Symmetrical where it should be, and yet casual enough to be welcoming."

"She is gifted. As are you, son. You may say you only built a potting shed, but your craftsmanship shows. Your attention to detail. That little building will serve Bridgeview for many decades to come."

"Thank you."

"I'm not saying it to make you feel better. You have talent."

Logan hung his head. How was a guy supposed to reply to that?

"So. Linnea. We've established that she's amazing and talented. Lots of people are. What makes her special?"

"I thought she was fragile. That I'd need to be careful not to hurt her. I never expected to... to fall for her and be the one getting hurt. She refuses to tell me what I did wrong, other than apparently not explain things to her. But how can I explain things I don't even understand myself?"

"Things like..."

"Feelings. Emotions."

"Are you talking about love?"

Logan scratched his neck. "If I knew, I'd tell her."

"Okay, so let me get this straight. You have feelings for her, but you're not sure what they are. She wants you to tell her them anyway."

Use your words, she'd shot at him. *Why did you kiss me?*

Why did a man kiss any woman? He'd thought the answer obvious. Uh, yeah. Obvious to a Neanderthal. Without words, why would she think he had anything but sex on the brain? But she knew him better than that. She should have trusted him. But she wanted words. Words that cherished her. Words of love.

Logan angled his head toward Ray. "How do you know when you're in love?"

He half-expected the man to laugh, even if sympathetically, but he didn't. "As opposed to being in like or in lust?"

Heat burned on Logan's cheeks. "Yeah."

"If it's just lust, the answer is pretty easy, I think. All you care about then is sex. How she makes you feel, not how she feels. Not about honoring her or making her happy. Not about pleasing God in your relationship."

Logan nodded. So far so good.

"As for when like tips into love, that's harder. Sometimes it sneaks up on you when you least expect it. It's when you can't imagine your life without her. When your thoughts are consumed by bringing a smile to her face. When nothing matters but her happiness."

Silence reigned for a few minutes while Logan absorbed those words. "And then what? I mean, if you think that describes your feelings, what happens next?"

"Then you pray, son. Assuming as one who follows our Lord, you already have been praying for her. About your relationship."

"Yes. I don't feel I've been getting any answers, though."

"Maybe it depends on how you're asking? Does your heart truly want God's best, or are you certain what that is?"

Logan rubbed both hands through his hair. He'd been making demands in anger, much like he'd kissed Linnea after Adriana's party. That had been frustration speaking, not love. It had been a last ditch effort to keep her from closing him out, and it had backfired.

Good job, Dermott.

"Let me pray for you, son."

Chapter 15

ALEX OPENED THE CAR DOOR for Linnea back at the apartment. "I had a good time tonight." His voice was low and intimate. "I hope you did, too."

Linnea swallowed hard. "I did, thanks." It wasn't a total lie. She'd never been to the symphony before and found it fascinating. Alex had treated her like royalty all evening, and she'd rubbed elbows with women in actual evening gowns. Thankfully her pink swirly dress hadn't been too out of place.

He took her hand and helped her out of the car, not that she needed assistance. "Maybe we can do it again sometime soon."

Her mouth dried and she tried to shift away, but Alex didn't release her. Give this guy a little encouragement and look what happened. Yet hadn't she decided he was a better fit than Logan? Oh, she wasn't likely to lose her heart to Alex, but what if the reverse happened? She hadn't even thought of that when she'd said yes. What a mess. "Maybe."

Alex slid his arms around her waist and drew her near. He was a bit shorter than Logan. Less muscular, but then pushing calculator buttons wouldn't build the same biceps as swinging a hammer. He smelled like some fancy cologne with not the slightest hint of sawdust or garden dirt.

"You've made me very happy today, Linnea."

Panic welled up. She placed her hands on his chest to push him away, but she was too late. Already his lips had found hers. She let it happen, but found it no more thrilling than bumping shoulders with a random stranger. Alex deepened the kiss, and then she did pull back and turn away. No. She wasn't ready for this. Couldn't do it.

Alex pressed her cheek against his chest and slid his other hand down her back.

She shivered, but not with pleasure.

"It's a little cool out. I'll walk you up." He kept her close to his side as they strolled toward the apartment building and up the stairs. At the door, he gave her a shy grin. "Excuse me for not coming in. My sister isn't on my list of people to end the evening with. I'd rather carry this memory home with me." He brushed his lips against hers. "Have sweet dreams. I know I will."

Linnea stayed still, listening to his footsteps fade as he took the steps two at a time. She took a deep breath and reached for the handle only to have it pull away from her touch.

Jasmine stood in the doorway.

Linnea's hands flew to cover her cheeks. "Oh, you surprised me."

"Sorry, I didn't mean to. Where's Alex? Didn't he walk you to the door? I was going to ask him something."

"Yes, he did. He just left."

Jasmine peered down the stairwell. "Guess I'll catch him tomorrow, then. Did you have fun?" She headed back into the apartment.

No wonder Alex hadn't wanted to come in. He thought something magical had happened and wanted to savor it. All Linnea heard inside her head was anguished clanging and screaming. She stumbled in behind her roommate, shut the door, then bent to undo the clasps on her heels.

"Linnea?"

"Yes, it was fun." Good, she'd kept her voice steady.

Jasmine sighed. "What did my brother do now?"

"Nothing to be concerned about, really. It was a first date. Nothing unusual." Seriously? Since when was she a connoisseur of first dates? This was the second one in her entire life. There was no comparing anything Alex did with Logan. That wasn't true. She'd been comparing them all evening, even when she didn't want to. *Especially* when she didn't want to, like when Alex had kissed her.

Yuck. How could she have let this happen?

"So he was a gentleman? 'Cause Dad will have his hide if he wasn't."

Now the entire Santoro family would be discussing her date with Alex? Dissecting it? Would Alex tell everyone he'd kissed her and she'd responded with the enthusiasm of a dead fish? No. A man wouldn't likely divulge anything that didn't make him look good.

"Alex was fine. I'm just tired is all. It's been a busy week at work. Dad's pushing hard to start prepping all the yards we work on for the winter, plus I've put in long hours at your grandmother's lot." She faked a yawn, but it turned into a real one.

"You've been going to Nonna's before work." Jasmine hopped up to sit on the kitchen counter, putting her closer to eye level. "Now you went out with my little brother. I can't help but think you and Logan must have had a doozy of a fight."

With the world's most divine kiss in the middle of it. Linnea took a few steps toward her bedroom. "Logan doesn't know what he wants."

"Do you?"

At her roommate's quiet question, Linnea whirled. "What do you mean?"

"Did you go out with Alex to get even with Logan? Because that's not playing fair."

"No, I did not. I went out with Alex because he asked me and I wanted to go. It had nothing to do with Logan. As far as I know, Logan has no idea I had a date tonight, and I'm not going to be the one to tell him." She raised her eyebrows. "Are you?"

Jasmine held up both hands. "I won't make a point of it. But I hate to see you using my brother on the rebound."

If only the color of her cheeks didn't give her away every time. "I'm not using him."

"Then what are you doing?"

"Did it ever occur to you that someone might find Alex attractive? To you, he's just a kid brother, but no one else sees him that way."

"I notice the person who finds Alex attractive is hypothetical." Jasmine's eyes narrowed. "Do you, personally, find Alex attractive?"

Busted. "I'm not sure."

Her roommate's eyebrows went up.

"Look, it's complicated, okay? But I'm not trying to play games with him. That's the honest truth."

"Explain."

"Logan is exasperating. I have no idea what he wants. One day I'm sure we're getting somewhere and the next, he's backed right off. So I'm done with that. I can't handle the drama in my life. Not with working for my dad and finishing your grandmother's garden. So that's it. I'm done with Logan."

"Instead, you'll put Alex through the same thing? Warm one minute and cold the next? Maybe the problem's not with Logan. Maybe it's with you."

Linnea stared at her roommate. "I can't believe you just said that."

"Sorry. I wasn't trying to offend you. But sometimes, when the same thing keeps happening, you have to look at the common denominator."

"If you're asking me to move out, just say so."

"Would you stop jumping to conclusions? Did I say anything at all about where we live?"

"No, but..."

Jasmine slid off the counter and took a few steps closer. "Life is full of compartments, Linnea. Your relationship with my brother doesn't have to affect us rooming together. You and I are friends. That's a separate box, and a true friend is going to speak the truth in love. We've been sharing this apartment for three months now. I've seen you floating on air. I've seen you nervous, sad, and angry. As a friend, is it wrong for me to point that out?"

"I'm sorry for over-reacting." Linnea sidled a bit closer to her bedroom door.

"Are you just saying that to shut me up?"

"Would it work?"

Jasmine cracked a grin. "Not likely."

"That's what I thought. Good night, Jasmine. Thank you." *I think.* Linnea closed her bedroom door behind her and fell backward onto her bed, staring at the ceiling. Maybe Alex would have sweet dreams, but she wasn't likely to sleep a wink.

ᡐ᠆ᢞᡈ

Pastor Tomas must've been seeing inside his head. From Hillsong's *I Surrender* to the old hymn *I Surrender All*, Logan's fingers and voice took him through the whole gamut of emotional responses to the Lord that Sunday morning. He was shaking when he took his seat next to Jacob. If Linnea was somewhere in the building, he hadn't seen her, but then, he'd tried very hard not to look. They'd sat together so many weeks in a row that no doubt tongues were already wagging. They'd only wag more if he seemed to be looking for her from the baby grand at the front.

"Let's turn to the first chapter of Colossians," Pastor Tomas said, setting his large black Bible on the podium. "We'll be looking at the first fourteen verses today from the New Living Translation. There's a copy in the back of the pew in front of you, or you may find it on your phone or tablet." He grinned out at the congregation from behind his glasses. "Only do stay off Facebook, please."

Jacob opened a pew Bible and shared it with Eden while Logan opened the Bible app on his phone. He followed along as Tomas read the apostle Paul's introduction and the prayer he had for the church at Colossae, but Logan's attention snagged on the ninth verse.

"So we have not stopped praying for you since we first heard about you. We ask God to give you complete knowledge of his will and to give you spiritual wisdom and understanding. Then the way you live will always honor and please the Lord, and your lives will produce every kind of good fruit. All the while, you will grow as you learn to know God better and better."

This. This was way more important than whether his dad ever spoke to him again or not. Whether Linnea's smile would ever light his life again or not. How could he even think about being in a relationship when he wasn't tuned in tight to God? No wonder she'd given up on him. He'd been acting like a kid, not an adult. That the parental figures in his life hadn't modeled mature behavior to him only went so far as an excuse.

Logan leaned forward, elbows on his knees, and cradled his head in his hands. *Lord, forgive me. I made it all about me. Not about Linnea. Not about You. Teach me. I want to grow and do this right.*

He could only hope he was a quick learner. Whatever Pastor Tomas said for the remainder of the sermon mostly zipped past Logan's head, but he snapped to attention when he slid back onto the piano bench for the closing song, Hillsong's *Heart of Worship*. The lyrics perfectly represented the cry of his heart. After the benediction, he played through the song twice more, quietly, as churchgoers slipped out of the pews and into the foyer. *Amen. So be it, Lord. All about You.*

When he finally made his way out of the sanctuary, Jacob and Eden had already left. So had most of the other singles, Hailey included. Whew. Alex Santoro took a step toward him, but Jasmine touched her brother's arm and said something. With another glance Logan's way, the siblings left the building.

Logan had half-feared Linnea might be somewhere with Alex. He could breathe a sigh of relief that at least that wasn't the case.

"Come for lunch, Logan?" Pastor Tomas's hand rested on his arm.

"Thanks, but not today."

"You seem rather thoughtful today. I'd be happy to visit if you like."

"No, that's all right. I do appreciate it, though."

"If you're sure."

Logan nodded. "I'm sure."

Chapter 16

*L*INNEA CROUCHED IN THE BUTTERFLY garden at Manito Park and lifted a milkweed leaf.

She caught her breath. There. A monarch chrysalis. This little beauty would migrate to California and warmer climes soon, unlike the season's earlier generations who lived their entire short lives right here. Was there a lesson to be learned from the life cycle of butterflies?

The sun might be shining, but the air was so much cooler than it had been last time she was here. With Logan. The first time he'd kissed her. She'd thought he meant it when it happened, but she'd been wrong.

Why were men so hard to understand? Look at Dad, expecting to control everyone around him by the sheer force of his will. Dave Junior was just like him. It was surprising they got along so well. Maybe her other brother, Dan, had figured there was only so much room in one family for alpha males, but did that mean he had to sell used cars and live in a cramped apartment with Dixie and her two kids?

And then Alex. Her roommate had been right last night. Linnea was using him. It wasn't fair to date him when he thought she might come to love him, and she knew she wouldn't. He was a really nice guy, but it wasn't going to work.

Logan. Why had he moved to Spokane, anyway? How much simpler her life would be if they'd never met. She'd probably still be living at home. She glanced over at the milkweed plant. Wouldn't that have been like being a caterpillar forever? Because right now, she felt cramped on every side. There was no place to turn to escape these feelings. That caterpillar stuck to the leaf must've felt the same way as the silken bonds of its chrysalis formed around it. Locked in it for a painful metamorphosis.

Yeah, she could relate. In her life, though, no guarantees existed that she'd emerge as a butterfly. Would God allow her to stay trapped this way forever?

Linnea sank back on her heels. Other autumn flowers in vivid colors and sweet scents surrounded her, the chilly breeze she'd felt earlier blocked by the protective hedges. Nature had an innate rhythm designed by the Creator. Had He formed humans the same way?

All her prayers lately had been reactionary while she careened from one emotion to the next. What had happened to truly seeking God? To centering herself in His love?

She closed her eyes, lifting her face to the warmth of the autumn sun. *I'm sorry, Lord.*

"I thought I might find you here."

That was not God's voice in reply. Linnea's eyes sprang open.

Logan stood a few feet away, hands shoved into the pockets of his jeans and a light gray hoodie covering his torso. The uncertain expression on his face was unfamiliar.

"Logan?"

A grin flashed across his face, but the dimple disappeared just as quickly. "I was worried about you when I didn't see you in church."

Only then? "I couldn't."

His eyebrows rose.

"I needed time alone. To think. To pray."

He rocked back on his heels. "I should leave you to it, then."

"Yeah." It wasn't what she wanted, but she couldn't tell him she wanted him to hold her tight, kiss her, and whisper words of love. Not if he didn't mean them. No, she was going to ground herself in God first and foremost. No more looking to a man to fill a need only God could satisfy.

"I heard something after church today."

Linnea's jaw tightened. "Oh?"

"That you went to the symphony with Alex Santoro last night."

She should've known someone would blab. Jasmine, maybe. She nodded.

Logan's expression didn't change. "Why? I thought you didn't like him."

I don't! The words nearly exploded from her lips. "I'm not sure how I feel about him."

"Sort of how you don't know how you feel about me?"

Oh, that was a low blow. She knew exactly how she felt about Logan Dermott. The only question was how he felt about her. Right now that seemed to be summed up in jealousy. "Why don't you go first?"

He blinked. "What?"

Linnea folded her arms across her chest. "Tell me how you feel."

149

Logan eyed her warily. "The same as I did last week when you yelled at me."

"I feel the same about you as I did that night, too." Confused. But that was going to end. She was going to bury herself in God's word and ignore men completely: Logan and Alex alike. She might even become a nun.

Okay, that was going a bit far. But no more being yanked this way and that on every whim of the wind. She couldn't take it.

Logan shifted from one foot to the other.

She'd never thought to see him unsure of himself. Maybe she'd had more of an impact on him than it seemed sometimes. "I'm not going to date anymore."

He took a step closer, his eyes widening. "You're *what?*"

"Not for a while. I need some space. Please, Logan. It's not you. It's not Alex. I just need time." Jasmine was two years older and wasn't looking for a man. She could be like her roommate. Carve her own future and be patient.

"But—"

"I mean it."

"There's something you need to know."

Linnea raised her eyebrows.

"Marietta has signed us up for a one-day permaculture course at Green Acres Farm for the first Saturday in October." He held up a hand to forestall her. "It's not a date if you don't want it to be, but I'd really like you to go with me. Besides, Marietta has already paid for it."

"Without asking." Why did that not surprise her? "Or did she consult you?"

"It was all her idea. When Ray told me, it was already a done deal."

"She can get a refund."

"But why? It's something you're interested in. I know you'll be fascinated with Green Acres. We've talked about it before."

"When we were dating." Now she didn't really want to spend a day with him in Idaho meeting all his friends.

Logan took a step closer, his blue eyes intent on hers. "We could be again. I miss being with you, Linnea."

Tempting, but not while he used those words. She shook her head, not trusting her voice.

His forehead furrowed. "Come anyway? Call it a professional development day."

Call it an entire day with Logan. A day she'd spend tortured by his nearness and the fact that he still didn't take her seriously. He missed being with her, sure. He liked having a casual girlfriend. Someday he'd really fall in love. He'd kiss that lucky woman with all that passion Linnea had felt after Adriana's party. One thing would be different, though. He'd tell that woman he loved her.

Linnea was not that woman.

But he was right. The permaculture workshop was right up her alley. She did want to find out more about food security like he'd talked about. "Fine. I'll come."

His eyes crinkled into a smile.

"But it's not a date, so don't get any ideas."

"One. Two. Three. Lift." Logan eyed Peter and Basil. The three of them lifted in unison as they climbed several steps up each stepladder. They set the gazebo's roof structure into place.

"Holes lined up?"

Peter nudged the thick beam over a little. "You've got it."

"Perfect. Hold steady." He drove the first peg through, pinning the roof in place, then handed the sledge up to Peter. A few minutes later Basil had done the same. Logan would catch the alternating pegs on his own.

"Thanks, guys."

Basil dropped to the ground. "It's looking good, Dermott. You've done a lot of work here. Hope Nonna is paying you well."

Best not to answer that.

Peter threw a handful of grass at his cousin. "He's a volunteer. You know how cheap Nonna is."

Basil swung to look at Logan. "Seriously? You did all this for nothing?"

"I was bored." Plus, the thought of working with Linnea Ranta had been tantalizing. That hadn't worked out so well. "And it will look good on my résumé."

"Nonna may be cheap, but Dad isn't. I know he's been writing the checks for materials. I'll talk to him. He'll do the right thing."

Logan remembered his own late night discussion with Ray a few days back. Ray might be Alex's dad, but that couldn't be held against him. He was a good man. Logan shrugged. "I'm not worried about it."

"Lots of hours, though." Peter glanced over. "Hours you could have used to get better at three-on-three. Because you need the practice."

Logan couldn't resist. "Lots of people never play basketball even once and still go on to lead normal, happy lives."

"Yeah, but we need a spare for Hoopfest next year, and we need somebody who can actually play."

"I thought Alex was your fourth." It hurt even to mention the guy's name.

"Our cousin Tony is moving back to Spokane next summer. He and Alex and Evan will be forming up their own team."

"Peter's right. We need a fourth." Basil stretched out on the ground.

June. Would he still be in Spokane then, or would he be in India? Somewhere else? Best not to mention it. "Isn't there some rule about Santoros only on your team?"

Basil laughed. "We can't help it there's so many of us. Rob used to be our fourth, but he got tired of Nonna harping on him and moved to Helena. Then Alex stepped up for a while, but I knew we'd lose him when the younger guys came on."

Logan shook his head. "You guys eat, sleep, and breathe basketball? Don't you know there are other sports? It's even okay to watch instead of play."

"And here I thought we were friends," murmured Peter.

Basil shook his head. "Define those words. *Other sports.*"

"Baseball. The Spokane Indians had a pretty good season. And then there's football. Plus, I heard about one where guys chase a puck around on ice with blades strapped on their feet."

"You're funny, Dermott."

"I try." It might not be so bad staying in Spokane. These guys couldn't help being related to Alex. When was the last time Logan really had male friends? Or friends at all. He'd always moved on before anything deeper could form. Yeah, he had Jacob but, even though they shared a rental, he didn't see much of the other guy. These days Jacob was whistling while he worked on Eden's house next door. One of these days he was going to ask her to marry him, and he'd move right out of Logan's sphere into the unknown realm of marriage and then fatherhood.

Maybe it was something to consider. Surely Logan could learn to be a good husband, even though his dad had never given it a try. There were godly men he could learn from. Ray Santoro was one. Jacob's dad was another. Even Logan's old buddy, Keanan, had been married for a couple of years already.

Linnea had agreed to go to Green Acres with him. That was a good first start, right? He needed a do-over, just like she did. He'd do better this time.

"So here's where you guys are." Alex's voice came from over by the gate.

"Hey, bro." Basil waved.

"Want to shoot some hoops?" Alex didn't seem to be including Logan in that invitation. He looked between his brother and cousin, avoiding eye contact with Logan.

Peter turned to Logan. "Need a hand with anything else?"

Logan shook his head. "No, I can handle it myself from here. Go on. Have fun."

Basil sprang to his feet in one fluid motion. "Shooting baskets sounds fun. Come on, Dermott. You work too hard. Time to play."

"No—"

"I agree." Peter stood. "Besides, didn't we already tell you you need the practice? We'll come help sling shingles on that roof tomorrow after work. Alex, too. Boy's getting soft, sitting in an office all day."

Uh, yeah. Like he and Alex wanted to bond.

"Can you believe it, Alex? Nonna isn't paying Dermott for this. We can't let him be the only one working for free."

There was something backward in that line of thinking, but Logan couldn't put his finger on it. He met Alex's even gaze. What was going through the younger guy's head? Did he think he'd won with Linnea because of their date last Saturday? Had Linnea meant it when she said she didn't want to date either one of them right now? Did Alex know about her resolution?

So Alex wasn't the winner. Not yet, anyway.

Logan managed a grin for his rival. "I'd love to play for a bit. I might get lucky and block a shot or two."

"You're really not in the same league, are you?"

Double meaning there for sure. "You're right. I'm in a league of my own. If we're going to play, we should get going. Dark comes pretty early these days."

Chapter 17

*L*INNEA ROUNDED THE TOP of the apartment staircase and gasped at the sight of Alex standing outside her door. Waiting for her. Watching her without a word.

"Hi." She managed to get out the greeting.

"Hi." He stood between her and the door. Leaned against the jamb, actually, arms crossed. "What's going on, Lin?"

Why now? Why here? It was a huge temptation to jog back down those stairs and run away. But where to? No, she needed to dredge up some courage. "Would you like to come in for a few minutes? Jasmine should be back anytime."

"If you'll talk to me. I've texted you a dozen times in the past few days with no reply. I've called and gone straight to voice mail time and again."

"I'm sorry."

"Really? You don't look it. You look more sorry that I'm standing on your doorstep, and you can't ignore me."

Um. Yes. He'd nailed it. She gave him a wan smile. "If you'll excuse me, please, I'll unlock the door, and we can go inside."

"Fine." He shifted just enough for her to access the lock, the heat of his body sending chills through her.

She could trust him. She had to. It took three tries to get the key in position. *Help me, Lord,* she breathed, as she pushed the door open. There was no chance of shutting Alex on the other side. He was right behind her. She wouldn't have done it anyway. Would she?

Linnea set her purse on the closet shelf and kicked off her grass-stained sneakers. "Have a seat. Can I get you a glass of iced tea?"

Alex crossed to the living room and dropped into Jasmine's papasan chair. "No, thanks."

She poured one for herself, buying time as much as anything. But he couldn't be put off much longer. Besides, she'd like him gone before his sister returned. Linnea pressed her hands against the counter dividing the small apartment.

"I'm sorry, Alex. I need to come right out and say it. I'm not planning to date anyone for a while."

His eyebrows shot up. "Three days ago we had a great evening together at the symphony. As far as I could tell, we had a great time together."

"It was nice."

"*Nice?* What did I do wrong?" His face flushed. "Is it because I kissed you? It seemed the perfect ending to a perfect evening. I should've asked first. Is that what it was?"

Man, this was hard. "Partly, but not only. I shouldn't have gone with you in the first place. I led you to believe I might feel something for you that I don't."

Alex growled. "It's Dermott, isn't it?"

Linnea shook her head. It was, but it wasn't. "I'm not dating Logan, either."

"Then what the—" He bit off his words. "I don't understand."

They should all start a club. The Misunderstanders' Club. She'd be president for sure.

"I'm going away to college in the fall."

He blinked and pulled back. "You're what?"

"This isn't going to be my whole life, Alex." She waved her hand around the apartment. "I work for my dad with no hope of advancement. I need to figure out what God wants of me, and go out and get it."

"My wife won't need to work if she doesn't want to. I have a secure job and make good money."

Was he asking her to marry him? Instead of heat rising in her cheeks, she could feel ice forming. She swayed slightly and pressed her hands against the counter.

Alex shook his head. "This is not how I meant this conversation to go."

"Good. It almost sounded like..."

He surged to his feet and crossed the space until he stood at the counter across from her. "Linnea, I care about you a lot. I always have, since we were kids. I know it's too early, but..." His brown eyes searched her face as his hands covered hers. "I can't imagine my life with anyone else."

Linnea pulled her hands from between his and backed up a step. Then two. She rammed into the fridge. "No. Don't."

"It's only true."

"You don't even know me. Not enough." He didn't know all her insecurities. Didn't know her passion for flowers and butterflies and fountains. Didn't know what made her tick.

"I know all I need to. Linnea, you're beautiful and sweet. You go to the same church, so I'm sure we believe the same things. Let me take care of you."

Her head couldn't stop shaking. For that matter, neither could the rest of her body. "No, Alex," she whispered.

"I'll get you a ring. You can even pick it." Desperation tinged his voice. "We can get married at Christmas and save up for a down payment on a house. It will only take a year or two and we can be into our own place over at Kendall Yards or someplace else. Whatever you want. Anything."

"Alex, stop." She covered her face with both hands.

He rounded the counter and gathered her into his arms.

"No. Don't touch me."

His hands dropped to his side. "I don't understand. What do you want?"

"I want someone who loves me."

"What have I been saying?"

He sounded genuinely perplexed. Linnea edged past him. Air at last. She stood beside her bedroom door. She could get in there and lock the door. He wouldn't push past that. "You've been saying things about marriage. Not about love."

"Why would I ask you to marry me if I didn't love you?" He came around and stood beside the table a few feet away, fists clenched at his sides. "I can't even think straight, that's how much I love you. I didn't come here planning to tell you that, but it doesn't mean I don't mean it. That I haven't been thinking about it. Linnea, please."

"How many times do I have to tell you no? How many ways? I can't marry you. We don't love each other." At the moment, she barely liked him.

"But—"

Jasmine's dry voice came from over by the door. "Sorry to interrupt this romantic moment."

Linnea's gaze jerked over to her roommate. How had she not heard Jasmine enter? More to the point, how long had she been standing there?

"How about you go back outside and return in half an hour?" Alex's fists landed on his hips as he glared at his sister.

Jasmine glanced between them. "I don't think so. This is my home. Mine and Linnea's. It sounds to me like you've outstayed your welcome, little brother."

"We have things to talk about. We're not done."

Linnea straightened. "We *are* done. I don't love you, Alex. I don't want to marry you. We have nothing left to discuss."

He reached toward her and took a step closer, as though touching or kissing her would change her mind.

Both her hands came up. "Don't even think about it."

"Alex."

"Jas, stay out of it. Just because Nathan Hamelin was a jerk doesn't mean I am. I'm not a kid. I'm twenty-four, and I know my own mind. My relationship with Linnea is none of your business."

"Low blow, little brother. It's time for you to go. You don't have a relationship with Linnea. You have to hear her words and believe them. If things change, she'll let you know." Eyebrows raised, Jasmine motioned toward the door. "See you later."

He sighed and glanced at Linnea, but she kept her gaze focused past him out the window. After a moment he strode over to the door. It thudded shut behind him.

"Linnea, I'm sor—"

Linnea whirled into her room and all but slammed the door. Enough with everyone's apologies and sympathy. Where was the peace that passed understanding? It sure wasn't found in any man she knew. But then, it never had been meant to.

"We'll be running through the winter with a skeleton crew, Dermott. I'm sure I'll be able to fit you back on in the spring. Looks like a few new contracts coming up then, but with just a couple of minor renovations over the winter, I can't afford to keep everyone on."

Logan shifted the hard hat on his head and glanced at his boss. He'd known this was coming. He'd even planned for it. A trip to India was safely squirreled away in his savings account. Problem was, the exotic wasn't calling him. Papua New Guinea was different from Argentina was different from South Africa. India would be different again but, for the first time in his life, he didn't want different. He wanted same.

Not same, exactly. More like roots. He could do something else with that savings account, like a semester or two of college.

"Thanks for letting me know, Howard. What time frame are we talking about?"

"Should be done with this place the end of October or thereabouts."

Logan nodded. A few weeks' notice. That was good. "Sounds fair."

"You're a good worker, Dermott. Happy to write you a letter of recommendation if you want one. And I'll be right glad if you join us again come spring."

"We'll keep in touch." Logan removed his hard hat and scratched his head as he crossed to his car. He tossed the hard hat in the backseat along with his thermal mug and lunchbox.

Would he really stay in Spokane? The thought had been nagging at him for weeks. Maybe it was time to examine it. He drove toward Bridgeview and the rental house Jacob would most certainly be vacating sometime in the next year. For all the razzing Logan had given his housemate, Jacob had manned up and figured out how to make his relationship with Eden work, goat and all.

Once again, Logan was on the outside. Restlessness overtook him, but it wasn't travel he craved this time. It was a wife. A home. A family.

Linnea.

What if he stayed, but she married Alex? She'd said she wasn't dating him, either, but that didn't mean anything. He and Alex were in the same boat, outside Linnea's favor. How had life devolved to this? Vying with a man several years his junior for the love of a woman? The brother and cousin of some of Logan's best friends?

Maybe some music. He turned the knob on the car radio, looking for something with a solid bass beat. Instead, a man's voice came on. "So he returned home to his father. And while he was still a long way off, his father saw him coming. Filled with love and compassion, he ran to his son, embraced him, and kissed him."

Logan's hand froze on the knob. Yeah. Maybe if Logan'd had the same kind of father the prodigal son had, he'd know how to do relationships for the long term.

"Luke chapter fifteen isn't the story of a human father and son," the voice from the radio continued. "It represents God's love for us. He is the Father of the orphan and the fatherless. In fact, as Psalm 27:10 tells us, 'even if my father and mother abandon me, the Lord will hold me close.' So if you are a man or a woman who aches for a relationship you will never have with your earthly parents, God can break the chains. History is not doomed to repeat itself."

Logan clenched the steering wheel and blinked hard. Man, he needed to pull over and listen. Those stupid tears threatened to mar his vision. He veered into a nearby parking lot.

"If you don't acknowledge the wound — if you don't grieve for it by pretending it never happened — you cannot heal. Does this mean going to the parent who wronged you? In some cases, it may. But the pain does need to be acknowledged and brought to your heavenly Father. He is the only one who loves you completely and passionately. He is the one who weeps with those who weep. If you are hurting, God longs to wrap His loving arms around you and comfort you."

God? I'm weeping. Are You really weeping with me?

"Ask God to meet you in that place of pain. Ask Him to heal the wound and fill it with His love. The craving inside of you is hunger for that full relationship of a child with his Father. Won't you reach out to Him today?"

Logan fumbled with the knob as music welled behind the speaker's words.

"Linnea's got the right idea, Lord. She saw it before I did, that a relationship with You will build the strongest foundation for a bond between a man and a woman. Whether or not You've planned our lives to intertwine, I pray that I will become the man You want me to be. Take care of Linnea, God. My dad might've been absent, but hers wasn't and still isn't. Help her to find the balance of respect and independence."

He stared out the car window for a long minute. Then he sighed and reached for his phone. Somewhere in his contact list was a number he'd called only a few times in his life.

Chapter 18

"I SEE YOU FINISHED the gazebo. It looks nice." Two and a half hours in Logan's car with him. They couldn't possibly ride in silence the whole way to Galena Landing.

His hands twitched on the steering wheel. "Thanks."

Whose idea had this permaculture workshop been, anyway? Oh, yeah. Marietta's. "I'm serious. It's a work of art. I was expecting something more basic."

Silence.

"The design on the supports is really creative. I haven't seen anything like it, and I've seen dozens of gazebos." Linnea darted a glance at him, but he didn't return it. How she missed his easy grin and twinkling eyes. His dimple. "I know some people who would probably hire you to build them one, if you wanted."

"You think?"

"Of course, you've probably booked your flights to India by now. Will you be gone before the community center dedication?"

"No."

Linnea's heart hiccupped. All the praying she'd done in the past couple of weeks hadn't helped get Logan out of her mind, so she'd prayed for him as well as for herself. He seemed to be suffering as much as she was. Why couldn't love be easier?

"That's good. Marietta says she plans on offering a tour of the garden that afternoon and getting people signed up for garden plots."

"So she said."

The impulse to bonk her head against the window nearly overcame her. "Logan. Talk to me."

He shot a glance toward her. "I talked to my father the other day."

Linnea wracked her brain to remember the bits he'd said about his dad. "Oh? Did he call you?"

"No, I phoned him."

"That's great. How did it go?"

Logan lifted a shoulder. "I caught him on the eighth hole of a golf game with his business partner, so he was distracted."

Why couldn't Logan finish a thought without prompting? Maybe she'd just sit and wait for him to finish. They had two hours left in the drive, after all.

"I told him I forgave him," Logan said at last.

This sounded promising. "Oh?"

"He had no idea what I was talking about, of course. No clue he'd hurt me all those years ago."

"And many times since then," she said softly.

"Yeah." Logan's hands shifted on the steering wheel. "I realized he'd unwittingly formed my concept of what a man was like. Just in it for himself. I thought that was normal."

Her father, too. "Some are like that."

"My dad walked away to avoid confrontation. Yours is a control freak and thrives on it."

The conditioned impulse to defend Dave Ranta Senior rose and quickly withered. Logan was right. "I didn't see that for a lot of years. I thought he was just protecting me."

"Not sure if that is better than being abandoned or not."

She tried to think what Logan's childhood must have been like, knowing his dad hadn't cared enough to be part of his life. No wonder he didn't know how to deal with commitment. No wonder he erred on the side of holding back. If she were going to take that thought to its natural conclusion, it meant she was expecting Logan to dominate her like Dad did Mom.

Linnea shot a sidelong glance at Logan just as he did the same. Their eyes caught for a few seconds before he turned back to the road.

"We're both a mess, aren't we," he commented to the windshield.

"I don't think we have to be. My parents don't have a great marriage, and it shows in all three of us kids, I think. But not every family is as dysfunctional as mine. Jasmine's, for instance." Oops. Also Alex's. Would Logan pick up on that?

"Ray is a solid guy. Seems like a good husband and father. His kids respect him from what I can see."

Right, Logan had become friends with Basil. He knew more about the family than what he'd seen through Alex.

"When I was in high school, all the kids hung out at Santoros. Ray and Grace welcomed everyone. They must have had a dozen extras at times."

"Probably not much has changed."

"No, it's still pretty busy around there, even with only Evan still living at home."

The fall landscape rolled by outside the car windows for a few minutes.

"I didn't have anyone like that to observe growing up," Logan said at last. "The first time really was Jacob's family in Portland, but I didn't know them until his older sisters had already left home."

Linnea nodded. She didn't know much about Jacob, really. He'd seemed super serious when she'd first met him, but now that he was firmly in love with Eden, he'd lightened up.

"You'll meet his sisters today, as well as a bunch of other people. Couples. Families. My friend Keanan has been married to Jacob's sister Chelsea for a couple of years. They're expecting their first child in a few months."

"That's cool." Hopefully her voice hadn't shaken too much saying that. She'd held Rebekah and Wade's newborn daughter, Olivia, the other day. She'd closed her eyes and breathed in the sweet baby scent, imagining the precious bundle as her own for a brief moment. Maybe her turn would come.

"Some of the other people at Green Acres Farm had messed up childhoods, too."

Logan seemed to be talking to himself, so she didn't answer. Besides, she was a bit curious about the folks she'd be spending the day with.

"I'm not the only person whose dad ever walked out. Whose mother didn't want to be tied down with her kids. Some people can rise above their background."

"With God's help."

Logan glanced at her. "I could tell you stories about all the families there, but the point is, they've devoted their lives to God and to their farm. They hold each other accountable in a good way. I think you'll like them."

"I'm sure I will." Already she was intrigued by the idea of a communal farm with six resident families who grew most of their own food. Now that Logan was over his funk and the sun peeked through the gaps between trees, it promised to be a good day.

The morning's classes had been fascinating. Marietta might have signed him and Linnea up without consultation, but Logan found himself far more interested than he'd expected. The basic principles of permaculture made a lot of sense: caring for the planet, caring for people, and sharing the surplus. While he'd found it absorbing, the fun had come from watching Linnea. He hadn't seen this rapt attention since the last ballgame he'd taken her to.

He got in line behind her along with the twenty other attendees for lunch. Linnea struck up a conversation with Kiara, a young woman from Helena, Montana. Logan glanced around. He hadn't seen anyone he knew yet at the farm. The morning class had been taught by two women, Allison, who looked due to have a baby nearly any day, and Liz, whose brother, Zach, Logan had met a time or two.

A large hand settled on his shoulder. "Logan Dermott? I thought that must be you."

Logan swiveled to see the tall redheaded man. "Keanan! I was wondering if I'd have to hunt you down."

Keanan Welsh thumped him on the back, and Logan staggered from the greeting. "No, I have been slicing meat for jerky all morning. The work must go on. This afternoon, I will teach on crop selection for your group. There are several parts. Noel — do you remember Noel Kenzie?"

"I think so. He guides hunting and fishing trips into the mountains?"

"That's the one. He is our tree expert, so he will teach the first part, on what trees to plant for the canopy crops. My expertise is in the understory crops, then it is back to Allison and Liz for the lower shrubs and plants."

"Sounds good."

Keanan grinned. "I didn't think to see you here."

"I've been working on a community garden project in Spokane with Linnea." Logan nudged her, and she turned. "Linnea, I'd like you to meet my friend Keanan Welsh, one of our instructors this afternoon. Keanan, Linnea is a talented landscape designer."

"Nice to meet you." A faint blush tinged her cheeks. "I've only done the one garden on my own, really."

"That doesn't keep her from being talented," Logan said to Keanan. "Especially for someone with no formal training. If you get down to Spokane, look me up. I'd love to show off our project."

"A community garden? Those are springing up in more cities. I am glad to hear you will have one accessible."

"It's more than a garden, really. Linnea planned a bee and butterfly refuge, as well as an herb garden for everyone to use. I think the neighbors will make great use of the space."

Keanan nodded thoughtfully at Linnea, and she shot Logan a glance from beneath her lashes. She might be lacking the confidence to tout her success, but Logan was happy to do it for her.

"Really?" Kiara leaned around Linnea. "That's so cool. I want to do something like that. Today is my first real exploration of the concepts, and I must admit I'm fascinated."

The food line moved forward, and the women turned to pick up their soup and sandwich trays. Heads bent together, they moved off.

Logan accepted his tray. Should he follow Linnea, or leave her be?

"Thanks," said Keanan as he reached for his food.

"You're eating with the students?" Logan teased.

Keanan grinned. "Sure, why not? The cooks made one meal for everyone. Chelsea and her sister are serving the young ones inside."

"I hear you'll soon be a proud papa."

The big man beamed. "Sure will. February will be here in no time." Keanan lowered his voice, shaking his head. "I felt the baby kicking for the first time last night. Amazing. I hope you will experience this sometime, too."

Logan couldn't resist looking for Linnea, but she sat at a picnic table with several other women, all talking animatedly. When he turned back, Keanan gave him a knowing grin. "Is she special?"

"She is, but whether things will work out or not, I'm uncertain."

Keanan pointed out a vacant table and started toward it. "I must say, seeing a man with such itchy feet as yours at a permaculture course is of interest. Thinking of settling down, then?"

Logan rounded the table before taking a seat so he could keep an eye on Linnea without being quite so obvious about it. "It might happen."

"She must be amazing. Linnea, you said her name was?"

"Yes. She's been working in her family landscaping business since high school, but she's wasted mowing lawns. You should see what she's done at the community garden." Logan pulled his phone from his pocket and opened the photo app. "Here, look at these."

Keanan thumbed through the images with a little grin. "You've got it bad, my friend."

Logan paused, spoon halfway to his mouth. "What do you mean?"

"Sure, the photos show a garden, but there seems to be the same woman in many of them. Sometimes she is even blocking the view of the flowers." Keanan turned the phone off and set it on the table between them. "What are you going to do about it?"

"Do about what?" Did his friend somehow think he could magically erase Linnea from the photos? As if he would, even if he could. Surely even Keanan Welsh wasn't that ignorant about the workings of technology.

"About the woman. Linnea." Keanan took a big bite of his chicken sandwich.

As much to keep from having to respond as anything, Logan followed suit.

"She is a believer?" asked Keanan after a moment.

Logan nodded. "She is."

"No unwieldy skeletons in her closet?"

"Not that I know of." Unless one counted her father.

"Then what are you waiting for? Life's too short to go it alone when you have found the right person to share it with."

"You make it sound so simple."

Keanan chuckled. "It is."

"I might have done it all wrong. Might have blown my chances."

"Oh?" Keanan lifted a spoonful of soup. "How's that?"

Where to even start? "She reminded me of a newly emerged butterfly. Fragile, like she needed protecting."

"Protecting from what?"

"From me." It sounded so stupid, so egotistical, to say those words out loud.

To his credit, Keanan didn't laugh. Instead, he set his spoon on the table and gave Logan his undivided attention. "Explain."

Linnea still sat at the distant table with her back to Logan, her long blond braid swinging slightly as she leaned to talk to the woman on the other side of Kiara. He looked back at Keanan. "I didn't want her to fall in love with me and get hurt when I packed up for my next trip. Because I'm so hard to resist, you know?"

Keanan waited.

"It didn't even seem like a strange thought process at the time."

"And then?"

"And then I discovered I was the one falling in love, and she was tougher than I'd given her credit for."

The other man's eyebrows disappeared into his bushy red hair. "You're telling me she isn't in love with you?"

"I don't know. Sometimes I think she might be, but then..."

"Have you told her?"

Logan turned the sandwich around on his plate. "What if I'm wrong?"

"Wrong about your feelings? Or about hers?"

"Either of them."

Keanan leaned closer, his voice low. "Sometimes you have to step out in faith and stop playing it safe. Love is worth taking a risk for. When Chelsea figured out she was really in love with me, she followed me all the way to South Africa."

Would Linnea follow Logan anywhere? It might be more like him following her to college. Him staying in the USA rather than wandering off as his usual inclination would be. Keanan's situation had been an overseas missions trip he'd previously committed to. Logan's motives were more selfish.

"If I went to college, what do you think I should take?"

"Business."

Keanan replied so quickly Logan's head swam. "Business? Why would you say that? I don't think I have any inclination to work in some office."

Keanan nudged the phone over to Logan. "You built that gazebo and shed in the photos, didn't you? You've always been gifted with your hands."

"They're nothing spe—"

"You're wrong," his friend cut in. "They *are* special. I think you should go into business for yourself, building stuff for people. For that matter, Green Acres Farm could use a good-sized gazebo. How much would you charge to build one for us?"

Logan shook his head. "I have no idea. Are you serious?" Although it would be a way better life than building houses with guys like Howard.

"That's the best I could come up with off the top of my head." Keanan poked his chin toward the other table, where the women now stood, gathering trays as they continued to talk. "How would Linnea feel about that?"

Puzzle pieces snapped together in Logan's mind. "You might be onto something, man."

Keanan glanced at his watch and picked up his spoon. "We'd better get this food gone. It's almost time for the afternoon sessions."

Chapter 19

"NOW, I'M GLAD MARIETTA signed us up for this workshop after all." Linnea leaned against the passenger side headrest and closed her eyes. "Seven hours barely scratched the surface, but my mind is spinning with all the possibilities."

"Mine, too." Logan stuck the key into the ignition and turned it. Around them, other vehicles began backing out of the Green Acres parking lot and heading down Thompson Road toward Galena Landing and civilization beyond.

"You?" She opened one eye. "I didn't know you were into gardens for the sake of gardens. I thought you'd be bored."

He'd only come because he wanted to spend the day with her, but that hadn't exactly happened. Linnea had made new friends to the degree that several of the women had exchanged phone numbers so they could text each other. Still, they had just as much driving time as class time today, and Logan wouldn't make the mistake of wasting the evening ride as he had the morning one.

"I never thought a lot about having my own garden before this project." Logan merged the car into the queue. "Partly because I was always itching to travel, I guess. Partly because gardens seemed like so much work."

She turned to look at him. "I hear you. I didn't realize it, but I'd been thinking about permaculture yards more than food gardens before this. How to set up backyard living spaces that require the least amount of hands-on maintenance. Like mowing strips along flowerbeds so you don't have to get out the weed eater, too, to make the edge look nice. Or ground covers that don't need mowing at all. Plants native to the Inland Northwest that don't need additional watering."

Logan nodded. "That makes sense. I bet there's a demand for that type of yard."

"It's called xeriscaping, and if that college in Edmonds doesn't teach it, I'll find one that does."

He glanced over at her set jaw. How had he ever thought her fragile? He hadn't been looking beyond the admittedly porcelain surface. "So you're serious about college, then?"

"I am. I guess I can thank Marietta for that, too. She nudged me out of my comfort zone and gave me a lot of freedom to test my wings. And now I want to fly."

This confidence-exuding Linnea was far more attractive than the insecure woman he'd met several months before. He'd seen glimpses of it even before the first ballgame, though. Hints that there were fascinating thoughts and ideas tucked behind the curtain. Hints that the damp wings of this butterfly would dry and strengthen and give her flight.

Something stirred inside him. He was going to be there for her. Part of her life's journey. Maybe someday they'd go to India together. Or not. He couldn't even remember the rest of his list at the moment, but it didn't matter. He'd spent years wandering the planet, but now he knew he'd been looking for roots. For a reason to stay put. For a woman who'd keep his attention for many decades to come.

For Linnea.

Logan glanced across the car to fill his eyes with her beauty.

She'd partially turned in the passenger seat to face him. Her blue eyes searched his. "How about you?"

His mind blanked. How about him what? Had she been reading his thoughts?

"Did you have fun catching up with your friends there today?"

That he could answer. "Yes. Good to see Keanan again. Without him, I'm not sure when or how God would have gotten my attention. It was seeing Christ in Keanan that attracted me to faith originally."

"That's cool. For me, it was the open house policy at the Santoros, and that a lot of kids from the church youth group were really open at school about their strong faith."

"That's when you met Alex?"

She nodded. "And Jasmine, though she graduated before we did. She lived at her parents while taking her massage therapy courses, though, so she was still around longer."

Best to tread carefully here, but he was dying to know. "You told me you weren't dating Alex anymore. How is that going?" Logan held his breath, gripped the steering wheel, and stared out the front of the car.

"He asked me to marry him."

Her voice was soft, but the words still pounded in Logan's ears. Surely he'd have heard if she'd said yes. He'd have noticed if she wore a diamond. He clenched his jaw. "Oh?"

"At first I thought he just wanted to help me get out of my dead-end job, but it turned out he was serious. That he'd been thinking about it." Linnea fingered the hem of her coral hoodie. "It was awkward."

Logan dared to exhale. "You had me really worried there for a minute." In his periphery, he caught her glance.

"What do you mean?"

He clenched the steering wheel. "The thought of you and Alex together makes my insides shrivel up and die."

"Oh."

He shot her a glance, but she'd turned to look out the car window. Man, he'd said that wrong again, hadn't he? "I... care about you, Linnea. I want you to be happy."

"Maybe I'd have been happy with Alex."

Walking on eggshells had never come easy. There were fifty-nine thousand ways to say this wrong, and only one way to say it right, but... which way was that? He couldn't come up with the L word. Not when he had no idea how she felt about him. "I don't think so."

"Now you're an expert on my happiness?"

"I'd like to be."

She whirled in the seat and stared at him. "What is that supposed to mean?"

Logan hadn't expected to upset her. This seemed to be like all the other times, where he couldn't figure out what she wanted him to say. What would placate her and make her look at him with wonder in her eyes once again. It seemed so long ago now.

"I think getting a college degree or diploma is a way better idea than marrying Alex." He could have kicked himself. Why keep bringing up Alex? It was like poking his tongue at a sore tooth to see if it still hurt.

"I agree." She crossed her arms and settled back into the seat, her jaw set. "College it is."

"I've been thinking about college myself."

"Oh? What happened to India?"

"It will still be there if I decide to go later. But maybe it's time to start a career rather than wandering from one construction job to the next."

Her eyebrows rose as she turned to look at him.

"Keanan told me I should start a business building gazebos and such."

"I already told you that, and you said no."

Logan's gut clenched. She had, hadn't she? "I wasn't ready to think about it then, I guess. I wasn't ready to settle down in one place." Would she catch the reason he was willing to consider it now? *Use your words*, she'd said to him. He had to go for it. "I want to know if we can have a do-over. You and me. I care about you a lot, Linnea. More than I ever expected. More than I've ever cared about anyone."

She didn't say anything, but he could feel her gaze on his face.

He plunged in again. "It's always been all about me. No one else looked after my interests as a kid. But God has been showing me I can't keep living like that. I have to open up. Learn to trust. Learn to..." Could he really say the word? He swallowed hard. "Learn to love, maybe."

The silence stretched for a long moment, but he didn't dare look over. Had Linnea even heard those last words? They'd come out more quietly than he'd expected. He'd laid everything out in the open, and now it was up to her. She could either stomp on his heart as she had Alex's, or give him another chance. *Please, God. Another chance.*

"I guess that makes two of us."

Logan's heart sped up.

"I don't know how to trust, either. To be open and... and vulnerable."

"Maybe we can learn together. If we keep trying, keep talking, keep praying."

"Maybe we can."

                             ᗒᓚᓂ

Linnea grimaced as she parked her truck beside her brothers' vehicles. She'd much rather have spent Sunday afternoon with Logan than with her family, now that they were talking again. But what could she do? It was Dave Junior's thirtieth birthday, and Mom had gone all out planning a family dinner. It was irrelevant that her parents wouldn't go to the same effort for her or Dan.

"There you are, Linnea," Mom greeted her. "I need help in the kitchen."

Linnea waved at her dad and brothers as she passed through the corner of the living room, but none of them acknowledged her. A football game was on the big screen, after all. Some things never changed. She took a deep breath and dredged up a smile from deep within. "Hi, Mom. What would you like me to do?"

"Mash the potatoes, if you will. I still need to make the gravy and slice the roast and..." Mom's voice faded as she peered into the fridge.

"Sure." Linnea grabbed the masher from the third drawer. "Pass me the milk?" But Mom was already on the other side of the kitchen. "Never mind." She got the jug out and dribbled some into the potato pot then turned to hunt for the butter, salt, and pepper.

Why didn't Mom ask Dan's girlfriend, Dixie, to help out? Screaming from the backyard might be the answer to that question. Those kids were completely untamed.

A few minutes later Mom nodded with satisfaction, as well she should. Roast beef, Yorkshire puddings, mashed potatoes, gravy, corn, and a Caesar salad graced the table, set with the china Mom had inherited from her grandmother. A huge birthday cake covered with whipped cream and dotted with chocolate shavings took up prime real estate in the fridge.

Last year on her birthday, Linnea's parents had taken her for drive-through burgers. Must be nice to be the firstborn. A son. A rising attorney. Had Dave Junior ever done a thing that didn't make their parents proud? She shoved the thought aside. Maybe if she'd think of today as a family get-together instead of her brother's birthday party, it would help.

"Dinner's ready!" Mom called.

"Just a few minutes left in the first half, Mom." Dave Junior didn't take his eyes off the TV.

Mom shifted from foot to foot, glancing at the cooling food then at the men in the adjoining room. Dixie herded the grumbling kids inside and down the hall to the bathroom, where splashing sounds ensued.

When they returned, Linnea helped two-year-old Buddy onto a tall stool. Three-year-old Mandy climbed onto the chair beside him and reached for the gravy boat in front of her. Linnea covered the little girl's hand and nudged it away. Mandy scowled at her.

"C'mon, Dan," Dixie called. "I'm starving."

Dan rose and stood in front of the sofa, gaze still fixed on the football game. No one else moved.

"Dan, you know I'm eating for two, and this smells better than anything has in the past couple of weeks. Move it."

Dad's gaze swung from the sixty-inch television to Dixie. Dan turned toward the dining area, a flush creeping up his neck. Only Dave Junior hadn't heard, or didn't care.

"What's that?" Dad asked sharply.

"I was going to tell them soon." Dan glared at Dixie. "But you spilled it. Thanks."

Dixie shrugged. "Whatever. It's no big secret."

"Have you never heard of marriage?" demanded Dad. "If I've told you once, I've told you a dozen times. You're not living right, and now you're bringing even more disgrace to the family. Why can't you be more like your brother?"

That got his firstborn's attention. Dave Junior looked up with a big grin.

Linnea wanted nothing more than to smack it off his face. Well, that and give her parents a clue.

"Can we have dinner now?" asked Mom. "The food is getting cold."

Dave Junior turned back to the game.

Oh man. Linnea marched across the space, grabbed the remote control from Dad's side table, and pushed the power button. The room practically echoed with silence.

"What'd you do that for?" demanded Dave Junior.

"Mom called dinner." Linnea dodged his outstretched hand and strode back to the table.

Mandy scooped gravy onto her plate and the tablecloth. Dixie didn't seem to notice.

Linnea took the ladle out of the child's hand and moved the gravy boat. She grabbed a stack of paper napkins from the sideboard and mopped up the worst of it, accompanied by Mandy's wails. "Can we sit down now, please?"

"It's my birthday, and I wanted to watch the game." Dave Junior towered over her as he reached for the remote.

"Then you should have asked Mom for a different time or day. She's gone to a lot of work here. Have some respect."

Dave Junior's eyebrows shot up. "Me? How about *you*, you little twerp?"

Moving out of the house in July had definitely been the right thing to do. Linnea raised her chin. No backing down. "Have a seat. You can catch the game highlights later." She pulled out a chair across from Dixie and sat down as Dan took a place beside Buddy. After an awkward moment, Dad and Dave Junior sat as well.

Linnea glanced at her mother, who stared back at her, frowning. What? Mom didn't appreciate her help? Whatever.

Dad levered several slabs of roast beef onto his plate before looking down the table at Dan. "What have you got to say for yourself?"

Linnea breathed a silent prayer for family peace and God's blessing on the meal. No one was going to ask her to say grace, that much was certain.

"So Dixie is prego. You'll have a grandkid. I thought you'd like that." Dan dumped a blob of potatoes on his plate and a smaller lump on Buddy's. He glanced at his older brother then at Dad. "Thought you'd be happy with me for once."

"Proud of you?" Dad laughed. "You sell used cars and live with a hooker."

Dan jerked to his feet. "I don't need to take this."

"Daniel..." Mom said weakly.

Linnea leaned forward to catch Dad's eye past Dave Junior. "Dan's got a point, actually."

Dad stared at her. "Doesn't your church preach that people shouldn't sleep around? I don't see how you can stick up for your brother on this one."

"Yes, but—"

"That's a new one." Dad's hand sliced through the air. "Never thought I'd agree with the church on anything."

Dan slowly sagged back into his chair.

"Dan's right that you have always treated him and me as second class citizens. Only Dave Junior can do anything right. You've withheld your love and approval no matter what Dan or I have done. Dave Junior isn't the only one who got good grades in high school. I had a better GPA than he did, but was that ever celebrated? Was I ever encouraged to go to college and get a degree? No. Just him."

"Dan nearly flunked out."

"He was good at other stuff, but you never encouraged him in any of it. You want to know why he turned out the way he did? Because you drove him to it."

"Yvonne, tell your girl to shush her face before I make her."

"Lin—"

"It's okay, Mom. I can take the heat. I'm not the same weak kid I was when I moved out four months ago. I've had time to think about my life and what I want. I'm going to go to college and—"

Dad surged to his feet. "With what for money? You can't afford it and, no matter what you said, you're not smart enough. I ain't paying for it."

"Maybe you'd like to give me a raise?" Her voice might be steady, but the butterflies tornadoed around her gut.

"Maybe you'd like to get a different job. Maybe working for your old man isn't good enough for you."

"Did you just fire me?"

"That's right. See how far you'll go without me."

Linnea slowly rose and folded her napkin. Suddenly she wasn't all that hungry. "Okay. If that's the way you want it. I think I'll head back to the apartment now."

"You don't have a truck anymore. I'll take those keys."

Dan pushed out of his chair. "I'll give you a ride. Come on, Dixie. Get the kids together."

"But I haven't eaten..."

"We'll stop for take-out."

Chapter 20

"SO EDEN AND I are getting married in spring. I can't believe she said yes!"

Logan sat on the bench in front of his keyboard and watched his beaming housemate pace around the living room. "That's great. Where was the part where you thought she'd turn you down?"

Jacob chuckled. "You never know until they accept that ring. Did I show you the ring? I can't believe I didn't show you the ring before I gave it to her. Do you want to go next door and have a look?"

His housemate was blathering. "Uh, no, man. That's fine." Logan held up both hands. "I'm sure I'll get a chance to see it sometime."

"I got Fern to make it. Keanan's mom. So it's one-of-a-kind."

"So you got her to put a goat on it?"

Jacob stopped and stared at him. "Pansy's okay, but why would I put her on a ring? What would that even look like?"

"Kidding you, Riehl. Get it? Kidding?"

Jacob scowled. "Try being funny next time. You missed the mark."

"I'll work on it. Is Pansy going to be your flower goat? I can just see her with a wreath of blossoms around her neck, prancing up... well, you'd have to have an outdoor wedding, I guess. Are you?"

"Eden wants to get married at Bridgeview Bible Church. And, no, we're not having Pansy in the wedding party. That's just dumb, Dermott."

Logan laughed. He'd known this day was coming, but it was much easier to take than he'd feared, now that he and Linnea were giving things another try. He wouldn't mess it up this time.

"Where are you going to be in May? Back from India? Or do I need to find a different best man?"

"You... what? You're asking me to stand up for you? I thought you'd ask one of your brothers-in-law. Keanan, maybe."

Jacob sat on the arm of the sofa. "I'd rather have you, if you're around. You've been here for me through thick and thin. Talked some sense into me when I needed it."

"Wow. Honored, dude. Yeah, I'll be here, no problem."

"I hope that doesn't cut your trip to India short."

Logan shook his head. "I'm not going anywhere. I think I'll invest in a semester or two of college and learn how to run a small business. Maybe do some custom carpentry for folks who want something special."

Jacob searched his face. "That sounds like an awesome plan. Staying in Spokane, then?"

"Thinking on it, for sure. It all depends."

"On Linnea? She's good for you."

"We're giving ourselves another chance, yeah. But it depends on more than our relationship. She's talking about going to college over in Edmonds in September."

"A lot can happen in ten months."

Logan nodded. "It can, but I want to encourage her. I think it's something she needs to do."

"Do they have a business program, too? Do they accept married students?" Jacob's eyes danced.

"Yes to both those questions." Logan took a deep breath. "Scary territory here. This whole making a commitment thing. What if—?"

"There's always a *what if*. Trust me. Well, you know. You've listened to all my ups and downs with Eden the past few months. As my wise sister once said, anything worth having is worth fighting for. And praying about."

"Shall I tell Chelsea you said she was wise?"

"Don't you dare." Jacob threw a sofa cushion at him. "It would go to her head."

Logan's phone beeped with an incoming text, and he reached for it. Linnea? She missed him so much she'd text him from the middle of the family dinner she hadn't wanted to invite him to? He opened the app to read her words.

"Oh, no. Linnea's dad just fired her." He closed his eyes and shook his head. "Know anyone who's hiring?"

"Her *father* fired her? What kind of man does that to his own daughter?" Jacob sounded incredulous. "Especially to one who didn't deserve it. I can't imagine her not doing a good job."

"I've had the privilege of meeting him once. He's an egotistical jerk." Logan stood and pocketed his phone. "I'm going over to her apartment. Spare a prayer or two for her?"

"You got it, man."

Linnea paced the small apartment.

Jasmine, curled up in her papasan chair, watched her. "Hailey said they're hiring at the bakery."

"Yeah, I can just see me working for her. It couldn't be much better than working for Dad. She'd always be waiting for me to screw up."

"I don't think you're giving her enough credit."

Linnea stopped in front of Jasmine. "She thinks I stole Logan from under her nose, which is dumb. He never cared for her."

"She knows that."

"Then why does she glare at me every time I see her?"

Jasmine shrugged. "How do you look at her?"

"Huh?"

"I'm guessing the two of you should talk. I think you both are wary for little reason. Hailey's actually really nice, and I think she and Kass would be great to work for. The bakery and bistro is always busy, so they must be doing something right."

"I'm not sure I could handle being cooped up inside all day." Linnea resumed pacing. "I'm not used to it. I like the outdoors."

"There's not much available over the winter, unless you get a job clearing snow off the streets."

"I know." She'd done plenty of that with Dad. He'd have to hire someone to run the other Bobcat, at least if they had more snow this winter than last. He had too many clients to do it all himself. "Don't worry. I'll find some way to pay my share of the rent." She certainly couldn't move back to her parents' house.

"I know you will. If there's a hiccup or two, I can manage for a bit."

Linnea shook her head. "I have enough saved for next month. I'll find something." It would need to be within walking distance or a reasonable commute on city transit. The bus stop was half a block away.

The door buzzer sounded just as her phone chimed with an incoming text. Logan, in both cases. She pressed the button to release the street door below, her heart speeding up.

Jasmine rolled out of the papasan. "I'll leave you two to it."

"No, it's okay. We don't need that kind of privacy. He's here because of Dad's ultimatum."

A knock tapped at the door, and Linnea hurried over to open it.

Logan stepped in, his eyes dark and serious as he reached for her. "You okay?"

The warmth and strength of his arms holding her calmed her as nothing else had. "I will be."

"I can't believe he did that to you."

"Me neither. But I did challenge him in front of everyone, so I shouldn't be too surprised." She relayed the conversation.

Logan squeezed her before letting go. He took her hand and walked beside her to the living room. "Hi, Jasmine."

"Hey, yourself."

"I've got savings. I can pay Linnea's rent until she gets back on her feet."

Jasmine looked between them, a puzzled frown on her face.

"Thanks, Logan, but I can do it. I just need to find a job. This time of year there should be lots of options with the Christmas rush coming on."

"You'll need something longer term than that. A lot of those jobs are temp."

As if she didn't know. Linnea took a deep breath. "Give me a chance, please."

"Or maybe you could get into college in January instead of waiting until fall."

"I don't have enough saved, and it's probably too late to apply for student aid."

"I can—"

Linnea pressed her finger over Logan's mouth. "This is something I have to do myself." She looked deep into his blue eyes, warmed by the depth of caring she saw there. "Don't you see?"

He captured her hand. "Just because I see doesn't mean I like it."

For a second he reminded her of that evening when Alex seemed to think she needed protecting at any cost. She stepped back, pulling away from Logan's touch.

"Talk some sense into her," he said to Jasmine.

Jasmine raised both hands as she shook her head. "I'm out of here." She crossed behind them. A moment later her bedroom door clicked shut.

"Linnea..."

"Logan, please hear me out."

He studied her for a minute before walking over to the sofa and sitting down. "I'm listening."

She hadn't expected to test their newly revived relationship so quickly. "This isn't pride speaking. This isn't fear. I need to make a solid effort to solve my own problem before you or anyone else jumps in and takes over. Can you understand that?"

He nodded slowly.

"Besides, you told me yesterday you'd received a lay-off notice, too. So you can't keep giving me money to pay my rent when you don't have ongoing income."

"I have savings."

"I appreciate that, Logan. But I need to get through this myself."

He glanced toward Jasmine's bedroom door and lowered his voice. "Promise me you'll accept my help before you have to move out or stick your roommate with the rent."

She tilted her head. That was sweet of him, and she really didn't want to take advantage of Jasmine. But it wouldn't get that far, would it? She'd find something. "I promise."

"Okay." He patted the cushion next to him on the sofa. "Come sit down?"

"Want to go for a walk instead? I need some fresh air."

"There's a cold wind. The days of summer breezes are over."

"Are you afraid of a little chill?"

Logan grinned. "Not me. Just trying to protect you."

"Well, you can stop it right now." She reached for her jacket. "Come on."

Linnea breathed a prayer before pushing open the door to Bridgeview Bakery and Bistro. Jasmine had made picking up their order part of her weekly schedule. Linnea hadn't set foot in the place for quite a while.

"Linnea! Good to see you." Kass waved from behind the counter. "What can I get you today?"

She didn't see Hailey anywhere. Whew. "Hi, Kass. I see you have a job opening." She thumbed toward the sign in the front window. "I'd like to apply."

"You?" Kass sounded surprised. "I thought you worked for your dad."

"I did. But I'm looking for something different now." There was no need to go into details, was there?

"Hailey's interviewing today. In fact, she has someone with her right now. If you have a few minutes, you can talk to her next. I happen to know there's a gap in her schedule."

So much for avoiding Hailey. "Sure, I can wait. Are you looking for someone full time or only part time?"

"Full time. It's hard to believe how busy this place has become since we opened up a year ago."

The door chimed as several people came in. Kass gave Linnea an apologetic smile and turned to serve her customers.

Linnea took a seat nearby. Kass was good with people. She seemed genuinely interested as one customer ordered a cake for her poodle's birthday party. Linnea wasn't sure she would've been able to stifle a giggle. Something like this shouldn't have surprised her after working in so many rich people's yards and seeing their spoiled dogs. Two guys ordered sandwiches to go. By then, a businessman waited for a doughnut and coffee. Kass needed help, all right.

A door behind the counter opened and a young woman with pink hair came out, popping bubblegum as she passed Linnea. If that girl got hired before her, she'd know Hailey had it in for her.

Hailey glanced toward Linnea and gave her a small smile. She turned to pour coffee for the waiting man. When Kass spoke to her, she looked over at Linnea again. The businessman taken care of, Hailey came around the counter and sat across from Linnea. "Kass says you're looking for a job."

"I am. Jasmine mentioned you had an opening."

"Do you know anything about food service?"

Linnea shook her head and pushed out a grin. "No, but I can mow a mean lawn."

Hailey sighed. "I don't have any grass that needs mowing. What I do need is someone to work six to two, Monday to Friday. It's mainly counter service, which includes fixing sandwiches."

"I can do that."

"It's not rocket science, for sure. And we can't pay a lot." She named a figure a couple of dollars above minimum wage.

A couple of dollars an hour more than Dad had paid her. "That's acceptable."

"I'm surprised you're here looking for work." Hailey focused on straightening the napkin dispenser on the table. "I haven't treated you well in the past."

Better than her own father had treated her, but that wasn't something she needed to share. "I'm willing to move on if you are."

"Are you still dating Logan Dermott?"

"Not *still*, exactly. But we are dating again." If that lost her the job, so be it. She'd find something else.

"I was so sure..."

Linnea waited.

Hailey shook her head. "He never was into me. Maybe someday my prince will come."

"I'm sure he will." And maybe Logan wasn't Linnea's prince, either. But even the thought of breaking up with him again was enough to make her hands shake. God had brought them back together, hadn't He? If they kept focused on Him and on talking rather than assuming, everything would work out.

"Are you willing to start this morning? I could put you on for a four-hour shift, and you can fill in all the paperwork before you go home. If you want."

Linnea glanced at the clock. Nine-thirty. "Sure, that sounds good. Hailey?"

The other woman raised her plucked eyebrows. "Yes?"

"You won't regret it."

Hailey shot her a tight grin. "I believe you. Welcome aboard."

Chapter 21

"OOH, YOUR RING! May I have a closer look?"

Eden held out her left hand and winked at Logan.

Linnea bent over it. "That's gorgeous. I've never seen anything like it."

Logan leaned closer. After all Jacob's rhapsodizing, he was curious himself. He had to admit his housemate had outdone himself.

"Jacob had it custom-made by his brother-in-law's mother. You've met Keanan Welsh at Green Acres?"

Linnea nodded.

"His mom is a jewelry designer and artist in Portland. He commissioned her to create this for me. It's so special."

"It's amazing."

He'd better get Fern Welsh's phone number off of Jacob. His housemate had set a high standard, and Logan couldn't do any less for Linnea than Jacob had for Eden. Logan stilled. How soon was that coming? Did they know each other well enough to be sure? How could he ever find the nerve to tell Linnea he loved her and wanted to marry her? With blinding clarity, he realized he did. He wasn't a kid, not knowing his own mind. What was to be gained from waiting?

Well, this wasn't the moment, for sure. Not at the Bridgeview Community Center with over one hundred of their neighbors gathered for the renovated building's dedication. Not in front of Eden and Jacob and Jacob's parents, who'd flown in for the weekend to attend the event and meet Eden.

The lunch had been amazing. The community seized the spirit of the day and brought dozens of platters filled with food they'd grown themselves or purchased from local producers. The last of the forks clinked as everyone finished up the desserts.

He'd do potluck with this group any day of the week. He hadn't tasted better food since his last visit to Green Acres Farm.

The buzz in the room quieted as Ray Santoro made his way to the microphone. He took a moment to look out at the gathering with a smile on his face. "Welcome, neighbors!"

Dozens of voices called back.

Logan slid his arm across the back of Linnea's chair. She smiled at him and nestled against his shoulder. He soaked in the feel of her. How he'd missed her during the time they'd been estranged. He hadn't noticed immediately how incomplete he'd felt but, now that she was back, he acknowledged the wholeness. That fullness was not just the two of them, but he sensed God's pleasure on their relationship, making it sweeter yet.

He caressed Linnea's shoulder, half-listening to Ray's speech. The man went on about the grants the community had received, all the volunteer labor that had gone into the building, and the solar system Jacob had been instrumental in installing. He called out Rebekah and Wade and the food forest they were planting on public land by the riverfront.

"Next I'd like to thank Linnea Ranta and Logan Dermott for their hard work on the community garden. Would the two of you come up here, please?"

Linnea glanced at Logan, eyes wide.

Logan shrugged and stood, pulling her up with him. Ray hadn't called anyone else up front. What could he want with them in particular? He held Linnea's hand as they rounded the bank of tables and approached the podium then looked out at the arrayed neighbors.

"These two are new residents of Bridgeview." Ray leaned into the microphone. "Linnea is no stranger, of course, as her family lives over on Riverside Avenue, but Logan has only made his home in Spokane since June. Still, when my mother decided to remake her vacant lot into a community garden and asked Linnea and Logan to turn her dreams into reality, they willingly agreed."

Applause rippled the room.

Logan's fingers tightened around Linnea's as he smiled out at the group. Where was Ray going with this?

"They agreed to do it with no personal compensation. My mother expected a basic garden. Instead she received a beautiful oasis with a butterfly and bird refuge, a pebble fountain, a bee habitat, and a custom-built potting shed and gazebo. All of this designed from two masters who donated their time."

Linnea shifted uneasily. Logan felt for her, but they couldn't very well run back to their seats now.

"After we're dismissed here today, my mother is opening up the garden to anyone who wants a closer look. You might want to put your name in for one of the raised beds for next summer, or you might want to talk to Logan or Linnea about custom work in your own backyard. Or you might simply be curious. That's fine, too. Now I'd like to call my mother to the microphone."

Marietta stood and took the few steps from the head table to the podium. "Raimondo told me from the beginning that you two were worth wages, but I didn't believe him. I thought maybe I would allow you a free garden plot in exchange for your labor." She looked at her son who gave her an innocent grin. "But he was right. The garden is far beyond what I had hoped for. So I would like to give you this." She handed each of them an envelope.

"Thank you, Mamma. Thank you, Logan and Linnea. You may take your seats."

Applause rained down around them as they made their way back to their table. Neighbors smiled and nodded and murmured congratulations.

"I'm afraid to look," Linnea whispered when attention turned forward again.

"Me, too." Logan turned the envelope over in his hands. "Tell you what. Let's open them at the same time."

"Okay." Linnea tucked a pink fingernail under the flap. "Ready?" Her pretty nails were a side benefit of her new job at the bakery.

"Ready." He tugged his envelope open and removed the single piece of paper inside it before glancing at Linnea's.

Her eyes widened as she looked between the two checks. "Wow," she whispered. "Two grand each? I don't think we earned that much, do you?"

Logan slid his arm around the back of her chair again. "Not as mere laborers, probably. What she's really paying us for is being craftsmen. For going above and beyond."

"I feel bad accepting this." Her fingers shook as she shoved the check back into the envelope. "It doesn't feel right."

He glanced across the room and caught Ray looking at him. The older man smiled and nodded. "I think it's okay," Logan whispered back. "I think we earned it."

⌒ℓℓ

Linnea stood with Logan, Marietta, and Ray in the community garden as neighbors clustered around oohing, aahing, and asking questions. Maybe the money had been earned, after all. Everyone seemed to be thrilled with the results. She had to admit it looked pretty good, and would look even better next summer when vegetables grew in all the raised beds, the herbs were in full bloom, and butterflies flitted over the landscape.

Her cell phone rang, and she peered at it. Her mother? They hadn't spoken since Dad fired her two weeks before. "I need to take this," she murmured, stepping out of the lineup. She wedged one finger in her other ear to block the noisy group as she walked over to the empty bee yard.

"Hi, Mom?"

"Linnea, where are you? Your father had a heart attack, and they're not sure he's going to make it."

Her knees weakened, and she leaned on the fence for support. "Where is he?"

"Deaconess Hospital. Can you come?"

"I'll be there as soon as I can. Where will I find you? Have you called Dave Junior and Dan?"

"I've called Dave. Can you let Dan know? We're still in Emergency."

"I'll call him." Linnea closed her eyes and breathed a prayer. "See you in a few minutes. Tell Dad I love him." He might not believe her after all that had happened, but it was still true.

She didn't have wheels, but Logan did. Should she ask him to drive her, or ask Dan to pick her up? She looked over at the group by the pebble fountain.

Logan watched her with a worried frown. As soon as they'd made eye contact, he excused himself and jogged over to her. "Linnea? Are you okay? What happened?"

"My dad had a heart attack."

"Where is he? Need a ride?"

"Please." This was why she loved this man. Yes, she knew it now. No questions asked. No condemnation about Dad being a jerk. Just a simple confirmation that he was right beside her, whatever the situation.

"My car is down at the house. Want to come with me or wait here? Or do you want to take a minute to change into something more comfortable? We could be waiting for news a long time."

Bridgeview Manor was a lot closer than Logan and Jacob's house. Her mind quickly ran through the quickest route to Deaconess. He'd have to drive back this way regardless. "That's a good idea. Pick me up at the apartment?"

"You've got it." He took off at a jog.

"Are you all right?" asked Ray.

"No, my dad had a heart attack and is at Deaconess. Logan's gone for his car."

Ray frowned. "He could have borrowed mine, but it looks like it won't take him long. Don't worry about us. We'll be fine here. In fact, we'll have a prayer meeting for your father. Keep in touch when you know something."

Tears sprouted to Linnea's eyes. "Thanks." She hurried past the garden visitors and fled down the sidewalk to her apartment. Her hands shook as she unlocked the door. She stepped out of her dress and pulled on a pair of jeans and a soft sweater. Socks. Tennis shoes. On second thought, she also grabbed a hoodie. Who knew how cold the waiting room might be? She ran back down the stairs, worried Logan was waiting for her.

Wait. She hadn't called Dan. She thumbed on her phone and pressed his number as she leaned against the wrought iron railing surrounding the landing. In seconds she had her brother up to date.

"You're going up there now?" he asked.

"Yes. I'm just waiting for Logan. We'll be there in a few minutes."

"It will take me a bit longer, coming across the city. I'll be there as soon as I can."

"I wasn't sure you would, after what all Dad said that day."

Dan gave a short laugh. "He's always spouting off. He's still our father, I guess."

"Yeah. That's how I figured it." Logan's car rounded the corner and squealed to a stop in front of the building. "See you soon."

The ride to the hospital was filled with terse directions, as Logan had no idea how to get there. When they pulled into the parking lot, Linnea reached for her seatbelt buckle, but Logan's hand covered hers.

"Linnea, let's take a minute to pray, and then go in together. Okay?"

She took a deep breath. Hadn't she wasted enough time? But maybe he was right.

"Father God, I ask for Your hand on Linnea's dad. I pray that You will spare his life and give him another chance to have a relationship with You. I pray for her mom and brothers, that You will comfort them and let them trust in You. Lord, we know You are in control. We acknowledge that, and we ask for Your guidance in how we talk to each other and to the medical staff. Please take this situation and use it for Your glory. In Jesus' name, amen."

"Amen," whispered Linnea.

Logan swept the hair away from her face as he reached for the handle with his other hand. "We're in this together."

Chapter 22

THE WAY LINNEA HAD seemed ready to bolt into the hospital, leaving him behind, made Logan wonder if she'd ignore him once they got into the emergency waiting room. It didn't matter. He wasn't going anywhere. Ever again.

A pudgy woman sobbed as she ran toward Linnea with outstretched arms. Linnea stepped out of Logan's protective grasp. She held her mother and rocked back and forth as their tears mingled before leading the woman to a seat beside a young man who could only be Dave Junior, he looked so much like the father.

Logan nodded at the guy as he sat down beside Linnea.

Dave Junior narrowed his gaze and stared back. Somehow he lacked the intimidation of his father. While Dave Senior was solid muscle, the younger guy seemed to run to flab.

Linnea squeezed Logan's hand. "Mom, Dave Junior, there's someone I want you to meet. This is my boyfriend, Logan."

His heart sang.

"Logan, this is my mom, Yvonne, and my oldest brother, Dave Junior."

"Pleased to meet you, though I'm sorry for the circumstances." He focused on Linnea's mom. "Have you heard anything from the doctors yet?"

She dabbed at her face with a sodden mass of tissue as she shook her head. "They're doing tests."

"Can I get you anything? A coffee, maybe?"

Yvonne's gaze flitted to the closed doors at the end of the waiting room and back. "No. Thanks." She looked back at her daughter. "Why didn't you tell me?"

"About Logan?" Linnea tightened her grip on his fingers. "We've known each other for about five months now, working together on Marietta Santoro's garden, but it's only in the past couple of weeks that we both acknowledged our feelings for each other."

Dave Junior snorted, but Logan ignored him. First he needed to win over Linnea's mother. Her dad would be more difficult. If he lived. "You've raised a wonderful daughter, Mrs. Ranta."

"Please. My name is Yvonne." Her gaze ricocheted between them. "I happen to agree."

Dave Junior leaned around his mother, eyes fixed on Logan. "So what do you do for a living, pretty boy?"

The guy in the buzz cut was trying to intimidate him? Logan grinned. "I'm a master carpenter. You?"

"I'm an attorney." Dave Junior crossed his arms over his beefy chest, his eyebrows raised in clear challenge.

"Hey, that's great. Did you get your law degree here in Spokane, or where did you go to school?"

Dave Junior blinked. "Gonzaga University School of Law."

Logan nodded. "Handy not to have to leave home."

"We're so proud of Dave Junior." Yvonne patted her son's arm. "He graduated in the top half of his class two years ago and has a good job now."

The guy smirked even as Linnea's fingers flexed around Logan's.

"Congratulations." Top *half?* Seemed the guy's ego was easy to feed.

The street door slid open and a lean young man hurried in. Linnea surged to her feet. "Dan!"

"Hey, sis." Dan patted her on the back and looked to his mother. "How's Dad?"

"We're still waiting for news," Dave Junior said.

Dan nodded then his gaze settled on Logan. "And you are...?"

"Dan, this is my boyfriend, Logan. Logan, my brother Dan."

Logan stood and shook Dan's hand. "Pleased to meet you, but I'm sorry about the circumstances." Linnea's hand settled back into Logan's. Maybe it was he who needed the lifeline, even more than she did.

The doors at the other end slid open and a woman in green scrubs strode toward them. "Ranta family?" she asked.

"Yes," said Dave Junior. "How's my father?"

"I'm Dr. Nyan, in charge of Mr. Ranta's care. He seems to be resting comfortably at the moment, but it was a near thing. If you'd waited even a few extra minutes to call 9-1-1, I doubt he would still be with us."

Linnea swayed, and Logan wrapped his arms around her. She burrowed her face into his shoulder.

"It'll be okay," he murmured into her hair. "God's got it." He held her close while listening to the doctor's litany of how long Dave Senior would be in the hospital and how his lifestyle would need to change.

"Can I see him?" asked Yvonne.

The doctor nodded. "Two at a time, and for five minutes per hour only at this stage. I understand your need to see him for yourself, but my focus remains on Mr. Ranta's health. We'll be moving him up to Intensive Care shortly, but you may see him first."

Dave Junior stumbled to his feet and held his elbow out to his mother, but Yvonne turned to Linnea. "Will you come in with me?"

Logan gave Linnea a little squeeze and nudged her toward her mother.

Linnea gathered her long hair and tossed it over her shoulder. Then she took her mom's hand and walked through the doors into the corridor beyond without a backward glance.

That left Logan with the two brothers. These guys were as different as night and day. Dave Junior wore a white shirt and saggy black pants. Dan was attired in a ratty sweatshirt and faded jeans, with a Spokane Indians ball cap over blond hair that stuck out around his ears.

Logan wasn't certain either was inclined to accept his presence in their sister's life. Was he supposed to make talk with these guys who stared at each other with shadowed hostility?

"Sell any junkers lately?" Dave Junior sneered.

"A few, and some good cars, too." Dan stared at his brother. "You milked any little old ladies' estates lately?"

Dave Junior's eyes narrowed. "That was uncalled for."

"I could say the same." Dan glanced at Logan. "You?"

Logan held up both hands. "I haven't sold any cars and I don't even know any little old ladies. I think I'm in the clear here." Marietta didn't count as a little old lady, did she? He couldn't for the life of him imagine anyone milking her estate and getting away with it for two seconds. She was feisty, that one.

Dan cracked a grin. "So you're really not in the same league as a Ranta."

Uhhh. "I've designed and built a pretty cool gazebo recently, though. I guess that's my claim to fame."

Dave Junior snorted.

"Sounds like good *honest* work." Dan flicked a look at his brother.

"I'm honest." Dave Junior thrust his chest forward.

Dan rolled his eyes. "So you say. How'd you meet my sister, anyway? Logan, right?"

"Logan Dermott. Linnea and I go to the same church. She and I have spent the past few months creating a community garden over in Bridgeview, paid for by the Santoro family."

"Dad was mad at Linnea for taking on volunteer work." Dave Junior sounded smug.

"She's good at that designing thing." Dan glared at his brother.

"She really is gifted. You guys should swing by the garden and have a look. I think you'll agree." Logan would leave it up to Linnea whether to tell her family about the bonus check or not. It wasn't his place to divulge that information.

"Might do that," said Dan. "Something you ought to know, Dermott. Anyone who messes with my sister answers to me, you hear?"

Dave Junior snorted. "Now there's a threat."

Dan's chin came up. "I've got more muscle than you do, Junior. I could take you down in five seconds flat."

Oh great. Logan held up his hand. "No need to prove it by me. I have complete respect for Linnea."

"Too bad Dixie doesn't have a big brother." Dave Junior's nose curled.

Dan took a step closer, fists clenched at his sides. "What's that?"

"You've certainly been *messing* with her. Prego, she said."

"Shut up, Junior." Dan gave his brother a little shove. "Dixie and me are none of your business. I got respect for her."

"Hard to tell."

Were these guys really going to duke it out in the emergency waiting room? It was amazing how sweet Linnea was, considering the brand of testosterone that had flooded her home.

"Honey, you're the only one who can keep your father's business running. You'll do it, won't you?"

Linnea braced herself on the handrail along the hospital corridor. "Dad fired me." The father who lay nearly as white as the sheet covering his legs and torso. The father who lay unmoving with multiple gadgets hooked up to his body and an oxygen mask over his face. He didn't look so tough now.

"Oh, you know he didn't mean it. He was just blustering. You know how he is."

She knew how he was, all right. "He took the truck keys and never phoned me to apologize or ask me to come back."

"He doesn't really do apologies."

That's where Linnea and her mom were different. Her mom might sound a little wistful about her marriage, but Linnea wasn't going to marry a man who expected the world — and his wife — to submit to his every whim.

On the other hand, the bonds of family solidarity already tugged at Linnea. Mom was right. No one else could step in.

"I have a full time job, Mom. I just started there. I can't up and quit."

Her mother's eyes narrowed. "You went to work for Jordan Lawn Services? Or which competitor?"

"None of them. I'm working at Bridgeview Bakery and Bistro."

"You're a common waitress?"

Since when was food service so bad? It was honest work. "Not exactly. I'm behind the counter. But Mom, they pay me two bucks an hour more than Dad did, and it's not as physically demanding." Not that standing on her feet for eight solid hours was relaxing. "The only time Dad ever gave me a raise was when minimum wage went up. You know that."

Mom sighed. "Your father holds tight purse strings."

"He does. I'm not going back to work for him the way it was. I'm out now."

"It isn't *the way it was*. Your father is a very sick man. Didn't you hear the doctor? He might still die. Don't you think it is your responsibility—?"

"Not exactly, no." Linnea scrubbed her face with both hands. *Lord? Why can't this be easier?* "Look, I can take a few hours on Monday afternoon and call his clients. He had most of the yards put away for winter two weeks ago. At least it isn't the middle of June."

"I guess we'll have to take whatever you're willing to give. You leave us very little choice."

Linnea reached out and touched her mother's arm. "I know you're stressed about this heart attack, but please don't play the guilt card. It's not going to help."

"I'm not sure what's come over you."

"I've grown up. That's what's come over me. I'm an adult with a job and an apartment."

"Don't forget the boyfriend."

"You're right. I can't forget Logan. He's amazing, Mom. If you give him a chance, you'll see. He treats me very well." A whole lot better than Dad treated Mom, that was for sure. "I can't imagine life without him." If there had been any doubt in her mind before today, it had vanished like mist on the breeze.

Mom pursed her lips and searched Linnea's eyes. "We'll see. So you'll come over at one o'clock on Monday? I guess it can wait that long."

"No, I work until two, so it will be at least three before I get out to the house. I'll have to catch transit."

Mom heaved a sigh. "Or you could get that boyfriend of yours to bring—"

"He has a job, too."

"I meant you could come anytime and pick up the truck. Then it won't be such a big deal."

Linnea nodded. "Yes, we can do that. Maybe when we leave here today."

Mom pressed her hand on Linnea's arm. "You make sure that boyfriend is good before you get pregnant, you hear?"

"We're not sleeping together." Linnea jerked away. "I told you he respects me. We won't have sex until after we're married."

"Well, that's the right way to do it, for sure. Too bad Dan—"

"Logan isn't like Dan. He isn't like Dad or Dave Junior, either."

"So are you getting married, then?"

"I'm not sure, Mom. Logan hasn't asked me. We had some misunderstandings earlier in the fall and we're taking things slow. Making sure God wants us together before we make that commitment."

"God."

"Yes, God. Pleasing Him is far more important to me than pleasing Dad ever was. Believing in Him and trusting Him to forgive my sins has changed my life."

Mom shook her head. "Your father always said religion was a crutch for the weak."

"Dad's not right about everything. You know that. And this is one time I know for sure he's wrong."

"I wouldn't go that far."

Of course she wouldn't. She'd been brainwashed by over thirty years with Dad. "I'll keep praying for you. For Dad. For the boys." Linnea was asking big things of God.

"No need, but thank you."

Chapter 23

*L*OGAN ALLOWED HIS HANDS to roam the keyboard. Not that he was thinking about music, exactly, but it was a way to clear his mind. It'd been over a week since he'd figured out how much he loved Linnea. He needed to tell her, somehow. Did a guy break this into parts? Talk about love for a while and then mention the marriage bit weeks or months later? Or was it best to go for the whole thing all at once?

It seemed like poor timing with her dad still in the hospital, but maybe that was just his cold feet talking. Did he know — *really* know — that the love he had for her would last a lifetime? What about all those people who got divorced? Hadn't they once thought it was a forever thing?

If they weren't going to make it into old age, wouldn't it be better to stop now and walk away, before they'd said their vows and had kids? But he'd tried denying his heart, and they'd both been miserable. What was that saying? *It's better to have loved and lost than never to have loved at all.* But that was talking about death, not about falling out of love.

I didn't fall out of love with you.

Logan snapped his head up and looked around, his fingers stilling on the keys. Next the guys from the asylum would bring him a white jacket with very long arms and offer him a ride in their nice van.

I have loved you with an everlasting love.

"God?"

No answer. Of course there wasn't. Logan just had an overactive imagination, was all. His heart resumed beating. His fingers began drifting over the ivories again. Okay. He'd pretend for a minute that God had spoken to him with an audible voice. What was the message?

His love endures forever.

His fingers found the keys for the Vineyard song that riffed off of Psalm 136. Sure, it was talking about God's enduring love for the people of Israel. He got that. But was there more?

So now I give you a new commandment: Love each other. Just as I have loved you, you should love each other.

Logan bounced off the bench, reached for his phone, and thumbed on the Bible app. Where was that verse, anyway? Aha. John 13:34. And wasn't there something talking about men loving their wives as Christ loved the church? Because that was an everlasting love, too, even though the church didn't deserve it.

His hand paused on the phone. He definitely didn't deserve God's love. He didn't deserve Linnea's, either. Not with the stupid things he'd said to her. And yet, here they were, ready — sort of ready — to declare love to each other.

There were three options, really. Break up with her and leave for India. Pain pierced his heart at the very thought. No. That wasn't on the table. They hadn't come this far to walk away. He couldn't do that to Linnea. To himself.

Or he could let things drift on the way they were, but wasn't that the way to misunderstanding? Relationships had to grow and develop. Otherwise he might as well go for option one, the unthinkable.

He set the phone down and began to play. Aimlessly, at first, his hands roving the keys with no conscious thought behind them. His mind zeroed in on the third option. Telling Linnea how he felt about her. He took a deep breath.

She'd been waiting for those words. Waiting for him to say, *I love you.* So simple. So true. And yet he couldn't think of anything more difficult, unless it might be, *will you marry me?* His fingers stumbled for a few seconds. Yeah, that would be harder, but first things first.

Linnea removed the elastic band at the bottom of her braid and ran her fingers through her hair, unwinding it. Whew. She'd called all of Dad's clients and made arrangements to do the final yard work of the season for some of them. Good thing she'd worked for him for years and knew his schedule, as his record-keeping left a lot to the imagination.

Her phone chimed with an incoming message.

Logan. *Want to go for a walk?*

Clearing her mind sounded almost as good as spending time with Logan. *I'd love to.*

Meet me outside?

Sure. When?

I'm there. When you're ready.

Linnea couldn't help the smile that spread across her face. Things had sure changed with him lately. He was putting in a solid effort to put his feelings into actions. Her heart definitely responded to that new, softer side of the man she loved.

Oh, yeah. She loved him. No secret there. She could be patient with him. It was too late for a different way. The weeks they'd been estranged had squeezed the life out of her.

A few minutes later she stepped out of the building into the blustery November day. Brr. Good thing she'd grabbed her heavy jacket, as it was much colder than when she'd walked home from the bakery a couple of hours earlier.

Logan waited at the bottom of the steps. There was something different in his eyes. Something softer — more appreciative — as he watched her come down those few steps toward him. "Hi, beautiful."

Her heart picked up speed as she stepped into his embrace. "Hi, yourself."

His arms wrapped around her, bulky jacket and all, and tugged her close. "I've missed you." His mouth covered hers, and she reveled in the surging sensations.

"We saw each other yesterday," she said breathlessly a moment later.

"A lifetime ago." He kissed her again. "But today was my last day on the construction crew, so I'll have more time now."

They strolled down the sidewalk hand in hand. Linnea shook her head. "I won't, not for a while. I have several of Dad's clients I need to finish up with next week after bakery hours."

"I can help. Point me in the right direction, and keep an eye on me—" he waggled his eyebrows suggestively "—to make sure I'm doing it right."

"But you don't have to—"

Logan's loving look stopped her words. "I do have to. I can't have you working two jobs while I sit around and do nothing."

"But Dad—"

"Have you been up to see him today? He's still in the hospital, isn't he?"

She took a deep breath. "Yes, for a few more days." They'd moved him out of ICU Tuesday, but his discharge date was still up in the air. His stats weren't as positive as the doctors would like. If they acted less professionally, they'd probably send him home just to get rid of his belligerent attitude.

"Can I take you to visit him?"

Linnea met his gaze. "I'm not sure that's a good idea. He took an avid dislike to you."

"I think he'll need to get over it. I'm not going anywhere." Logan bent to kiss her.

The tingle started at her lips and ended at her toes. This was the closest thing to a declaration she'd heard yet. Maybe there was hope for the future after all.

Palms sweating, Logan stood in front of the elevator in Deaconess Hospital. He'd been here yesterday with Linnea, but this was harder. Much harder. Just because Dave Ranta Senior lay flat on his back on a hospital bed didn't make the man any less intimidating than when he was pointing a Bobcat at Logan.

"Lord? I could use some help here."

A passerby gave him a curious look.

Right. He punched the button to summon the elevator. A few minutes later he stood outside the ward, repeating the prayer, this time silently. He didn't need anyone else thinking he was a whack job. Definitely not someone who had the mental health department on speed dial.

Alrighty. Here went nothing. Logan entered the semi-private room.

Dave Senior's narrowing gaze swung right past his wife and straight at Logan. "What are you doing here?"

Yvonne turned and gave him a tight-lipped smile as she stood. "Logan. What a surprise."

"Hi." This had been a crazy idea. They hated him. He should elope with Linnea and move somewhere far away. "I hope you're feeling better today, sir."

Linnea's mom glanced between them. "I think they'll release him on Monday. He's already all worked up about the business, though."

Dave Senior's glare seemed multi-purpose. Maybe Logan didn't need to take it so personally.

"Linnea has everything under control. You don't need to worry about your clients." Logan shifted from one foot to the other. "It's not too busy this time of year."

"What do you know about it?"

Logan leveled his gaze at Dave Senior. "Not much beyond what Linnea has told me, for sure. But I'm learning. I'll be helping her wrap things up at the various sites."

"I'm not paying you."

"I never asked you to. I'm not doing it for you. I'm doing it for your daughter."

Dave Senior struggled to one elbow. "That's another thing—"

"Dave." The quiet word from his wife stopped him.

Logan took a deep breath. "I've known her since June. She's pretty amazing, but then I guess you already know that. In fact, I can't imagine my life without her, and I'd really prefer not to make her choose between you and me. I'm hoping we can agree to get along."

Yvonne's gaze ping-ponged between the two men, but Dave Senior's eyes never wavered. "You are not good enough for my daughter."

Would anyone be? Logan doubted it. "I understand, sir. The thing is, I..." Could he really say the words? He had to. "I love her, and I'm pretty sure she loves me back. I'm not perfect, and neither is she, but we both are trying to be more like Jesus. I think as long as we keep our focus on that, we'll do okay. More than okay. We'll have a great m... marriage. But I really want you to be okay with it. It's not fair to Linnea if you're not." He needed to stop babbling.

"If I told you to get away from my daughter and stay away, would you do it?" Dave Senior's eyes pierced him.

Yvonne's fingers tightened on her husband's arm.

Logan kept his gaze steady by sheer force of will. "No, sir. Not unless she told me the same."

"Will you cut your hair if I tell you to?"

"No, sir. Not unless Linnea asks me. I doubt she will, any more than I'd ask her to cut hers." If anything, he thought she rather liked his hair. He knew he liked hers.

"Then why are we having this conversation?"

"That's a fair question." Logan took a deep breath and let it out slowly. "Because you're her parents, and I'd much prefer both of us to have a good relationship with you than not. As I see it, it's your choice."

"Dave..." whispered Yvonne.

He shot her an irritated look then turned back to Logan.

Yvonne cleared her throat. "I don't want to lose my daughter over this. It was bad enough when you drove her out of the house."

"I did nothing of the kind. She chose to leave."

"Because..." She dropped her gaze. "Never mind."

"I thought that Bible of yours told kids to obey their parents."

"Linnea's twenty-four. She's hardly a child anymore. But you are right that we want to live by biblical principles, and the principle here is respect. She respects you, and so do I." At least he was trying. "I'm asking for the same in return."

"Not too many have been brave enough to stand up to Dave," murmured Yvonne.

Sounded a bit like he had Linnea's mom's respect. That was a start. Logan raised his eyebrows at Dave Senior. "What do you think?"

"You're not going to catch me going soft."

Logan waited.

"But, whatever. You kids do what you want. You will anyway."

Logan's heart sped up. Was acceptance enough? "Will you walk her down the aisle and give her to me on our wedding day?"

A sneer lifted Dave Senior's nose. "Haven't you taken her already?"

"No, sir. I haven't. I believe in sex after marriage, not before."

Linnea's parents exchanged a look. Yvonne's fingers smoothed the hair on Dave Senior's arm. "That's better than Dan and Dixie," she murmured.

Was that a reply? Not quite.

"I guess you got me cornered," Dave Senior said at last. "That don't come easy, I'll have you know."

Chapter 24

*L*INNEA HAD NEVER SEEN her father looking vulnerable before this past week. Seeing him tucked up with a white sheet, albeit with fewer hookups than Saturday, pulled at her heart.

"Dad?"

His eyes blinked open, and the perpetual scowl returned to his face. "Oh, it's you."

She sighed. That was more familiar. "How are you feeling today?"

"Ask your mother. She always seems to know."

Linnea pushed out a smile. "Mom's not here. Besides, I asked you."

"They figure on keeping me until Monday. Maybe you can talk some sense into the doctor and get me out today."

"No, sorry. I'm not interfering. The doctors know what they're doing."

His nose wrinkled in distaste. "They're conspiring to change my life." He took on a mocking tone. "You'll need to watch your diet, Mr. Ranta. Maybe meditation would help your stress level, Mr. Ranta."

223

Linnea perched on the chair beside the bed. "I'm not so sure about meditation, but I do know that prayer works wonders when I'm stressed. I give my problems over to God, and—"

"You got nothing to be stressed about, girl. Try running a business. Try living with your mother."

"Everyone has stress, Dad. Only Jesus can—"

"You sound like that boyfriend of yours. I guess you deserve each other."

Her boyfriend what? Logan hadn't said anything to Dad about Jesus the two times he'd accompanied her to the hospital.

Dad nodded. "He couldn't stand to see a good man down, but had to come here and push me further. All his talk about following God and respect and love. He's a sissy boy, if you ask me."

What on earth? Linnea shook her head. "I have no idea what you are talking about."

"You haven't slept with him?"

"Dad!"

"I'm your father. Just give me a straight answer. Are you knocked up?"

Linnea surged to her feet. "I am not. I haven't had sex with him or with anybody. I can't believe you'd think that of me."

"In your generation, everyone does it. Look at your brother."

"That doesn't mean I have or will. Dad, I love Logan." There. She'd said it out loud. "But he wouldn't ever pressure me. I know he shares my values."

"So are you going to marry the guy?"

"I-I expect I will, but he hasn't asked me."

"I wonder what's holding him back."

That smirk on Dad's face. Did he know something she didn't? Impossible.

"He's smarter than he looks, though. Sticks up for himself." Dad sounded grudgingly impressed. "I guess if you want to hook up with him, I'm not going to stop you."

"What?" Linnea's brow furrowed. "I'm confused. What are you talking about? I mean, that's great, but..."

Dad snorted and waved a hand. "Guess I shouldn't have said anything. He came to visit yesterday. Don't worry about it."

Logan had talked to Dad about marrying her? That's all she could piece together, but she wasn't going to ask Dad flat out. In fact, the subject could stand changing completely. She'd tuck this aside to think about later.

"I came to talk to you about the business."

He narrowed his eyes at her. "Yeah?"

"I think you should talk to Dan about taking over. It might be time for you to retire."

"I'm not sixty-five."

"No, I know. But the house is paid for and you do have savings. Plus, you could probably work for Dan part time if you wanted, but let him handle things."

"And let him run it into the ground? Not going to happen."

"Dan's made some poor choices." Linnea took a deep breath. "But he really likes working outside and doing lawn care. He's only selling cars because he feels like you drove him away. I think he'd be happy to step in."

"And tell his old man what to do."

Linnea sighed. "The whole world isn't out to get you, Dad. You have choices, too."

His hands twitched the edge of the sheet. "Sure don't feel like it anymore."

"You can choose to respect your wife and kids."

Dad's eyes narrowed.

Whoa. Had she said that out loud? In for a nickel, in for a dollar. "Attitude isn't about what our life is like. It's about how we choose to perceive it and treat everyone else, including ourselves. I'm not sure what, exactly, you're trying to prove, but it's okay to change. It's not weakness to be nice to people."

"Nearly done with your sermon?"

"Not quite. I've found that faith in God has made a huge difference to my attitude. I'm so thankful I started hanging around with kids from church after we moved to Spokane. I learned about how much God loves me and that He sent His Son, Jesus, to die so that I could have life. He loves you, too, Dad."

"You think Dan knows anything about running a business?"

Linnea blinked. Okay, she'd said her piece for now. "I know he does. He's managing that used car lot, but he always asked me about the lawn care clients when I'd see him. I know he'd appreciate the chance to do it."

"What about you? For a girl, you're pretty smart. You could do it."

"Thanks." She'd skip being offended by the sting in the compliment. "But I'm planning to go to college next fall. I love yards and gardens, too, but I want to design them more than I want to mow grass."

"Huh." Dad stared at her like she'd grown two heads.

"Want me to talk to Dan and see if he's interested? He could pop by and visit you, and you guys could hash out the details." If she didn't make them connect, they likely wouldn't.

Dad glanced at the monitors beside him and sighed. "Making no promises, but talking don't hurt, I guess."

"That's all I ask." Linnea rose. "Everything's wrapped up for the fall and final billings have been mailed. The folks who usually get us to do their snow removal are waiting to hear back from us on whether we're doing that this year. I'll give Dan a call, and we'll go from there."

"College, huh?"

Linnea smiled. "When you're out of the hospital, I'd like to take you to the garden Logan and I designed and built. You'll see why I'm so inspired to do more of it."

"Probably be snowing by then."

"No snow in the forecast this week." She leaned over and brushed her lips over his cheek. "See you later, Dad."

He grunted acknowledgment as she walked out of the room.

Her mind swung to what he'd said earlier. Had Logan really come to ask Dad's permission to marry her? She barely kept her feet from skipping on the way to the elevator.

How many years since he'd seen snow? Just the sight of all the glistening whiteness from last night's snowfall lifted Logan's spirits. He gripped Linnea's hand. "I'm trying to remember why I've spent my adult life avoiding winter."

She laughed, twining her gloved fingers with his. "I love snow. Everything is all clean and new, like a fresh start." The brisk air brought out the natural flush of her cheeks, and her blue eyes sparkled. She swung their joined hands between them as they wandered through Manito Park.

He'd been going to be in India by now. Never had a change of plans seemed so good, but he still felt anxious to get to the next stage. If only he could find the ring that matched the vision in his mind's eye at a price he could afford. The custom route his housemate had taken simply wasn't in the budget and, besides, Fern Welsh was booked with custom orders well into next year. Logan couldn't wait that long.

"What are you thinking?" Linnea's blue eyes shone.

How he loved her eyes. That one ring he'd seen had sapphires flanking the diamond. He adjusted his mental picture. Yes, that could work. If only he could find it.

"I'm thinking how beautiful your eyes are." He turned and gathered her in his arms. "Not just your eyes. Everything about you."

Her pretty mouth begged to be kissed. He swept his lips across hers, but keeping it light was impossible when she slipped her arms around his neck and kissed him back.

Logan groaned and clutched her closer, his kiss deepening with her response. He could drown here, deep in her love.

Love.

He pulled away slightly, but she pursued him, holding his face between her hands and kissing him until his knees went weak.

Somehow, he managed to get her name out. "Linnea..."

"Yes?" She kissed him again.

Logan caught her hands in his and stepped back. "Linnea, I need you to know something."

Her blue eyes shone, and her lips looked even pinker from the kissing.

"I want to tell you... that I love you."

"I love you, too, Logan."

He feathered kisses over her cheeks. "I love you," he whispered. It was easier the second time.

Linnea captured his lips again with a new urgency, but he couldn't keep this up without breaking promises. Somehow he managed to pull away and start their walk again, this time with arms wrapped around each other.

The crisp, cold air tugged at him, cooling his cheeks. His gut churned with relief that he'd finally gotten the words out. He meant them, for sure. She was amazing, and she loved him back. How had he gotten so lucky?

Not luck. God had brought them together, and He'd had plenty to teach both of them through this relationship. No doubt they'd keep on learning. Logan thrilled at the thought. This was all new territory. Being in love. Planning a proposal. What would she expect there? Were there rules he needed to know? At least the wedding would be mostly out of his hands. She'd handle that, right? Her and her mom?

His heart was stepping out onto a glass bridge over a deep canyon, taking him with it. That bridge would hold him up, but it still took a lot of faith.

After another toe-curling kiss on the doorstep, Linnea entered the apartment.

Jasmine glanced up from the papasan chair and set aside the book she'd been reading. "Cold out there?"

Had it been? Linnea felt more on fire than cold. "Uh, yes."

Jasmine laughed. "I guess the old saying about love keeping you warm must be true."

Linnea unzipped her boots and tugged them off. "It might be." After hanging her parka in the closet, she filled the kettle and put it on to heat. "Want a cup of tea?"

"Sounds good, sure. Whatever you're having."

"Once a long time ago you said something about me being in love with being in love." Linnea set her hands on the dividing counter and looked at her roommate.

"Yeah, I did."

"I thought about that a lot."

"Look, I'm sorry. I shouldn't have let my personal prejudice color my attitude."

"No, you were right." Linnea bit her lip. "I've never dated much, probably because I was afraid of how my father would treat the poor guy. So it was a bit heady having a man like Logan show interest in me. I didn't know how to handle it. And then the whole thing with Alex. I'm not proud of that."

Jasmine shrugged. "He'll get over it. He's a big boy."

"I wasn't trying to mislead him."

"I know."

"Because I know now what love really feels like." Linnea took a deep breath, unable to contain herself anymore. "Logan finally said it! I can hardly believe it."

Jasmine bounced out of the deep chair. "He asked you to marry him? Wow! Congrats."

"Um, no. He told me he loved me." The other couldn't be too far behind, could it? She'd waited and waited, hoping he'd finish what he'd started to talk about today, but he hadn't.

"Oh." Jasmine leaned against the kitchen table. "I didn't realize he hadn't said that to you before."

"It seemed to be really hard for him to say, but he said it several times today. I can't tell you how it makes me feel. Special. Cherished."

"I'm sorry for jumping to conclusions. I was sure you were going to tell me he'd proposed."

"No, not yet. My dad let slip a couple of days ago that Logan had talked to him about marrying me, so I know he's thinking about it. I'm trying not to be too impatient."

Jasmine's eyes widened. "He asked your *dad?* Wow, the guy has more gumption than I would have thought."

"I know, right? That took some nerve. You'd think it would be a whole lot easier to ask me than my dad. I wonder what he's waiting for? I don't think I scared him off..." Or had she? Had she been too eager to kiss him back? Though they'd been kissing again for a couple of weeks. Maybe she'd been too quick to say *I love you* back at him. What else could it be?

"Knowing Logan, he's probably planning some big extravaganza. Isn't he the kind who'd propose over the Jumbotron at a sports event or something like that?"

"He wouldn't!" Linnea clapped both hands over her mouth. She'd be mortified.

Jasmine laughed. "Anyway, worrying about it won't help. Just enjoy the journey. You know it's coming, so relax."

"I'll try, but you're scaring me."

"Sorry. And hey, the kettle's boiling."

Linnea turned to fix the tea. She handed one cup to Jasmine and followed her roommate into the living room.

"Hailey might be upset when you're flashing a ring, though."

"She'll be fine." Linnea settled onto the end of the sofa and set her tea down.

Jasmine raised her eyebrows. "You think?"

"Remember I work for her. She realized a while back that there was no use pining over Logan. Now she's pursuing one of our regular clients. The guy might not even be running away. Yet."

"Oh, that's good. About you and Logan, I mean. Too bad for the other man."

Linnea laughed. "Hailey is something else, but one day she'll meet her match." She watched Jasmine for a moment. "So will you."

"Oh, I'm not looking. Don't put me in the same boat as Hailey."

"There's more than one boat."

Chapter 25

"HEY, WE HAVEN'T BEEN here in a while." Logan steered Linnea into the community garden. It was covered in a swath of white. The frost on the grasses reminded him of lace on a bridal gown. He'd take that as a good sign.

"I love winter." Linnea sighed, her eyes crinkling with a happy smile. "But I can't wait to see this place alive again. Flowers, birds, butterflies. Even bees."

"Neighbors chatting as they dig in their garden beds," added Logan.

"That, too. I'll really miss this place when I go away to school."

"About that. Are you sure you want to?"

She looked over at him. "Yeah, I really do."

"I've been looking into business courses at a variety of colleges. A friend of Ray's contacted me to craft a portico for him come spring, and I've had a couple of other inquiries, too."

"That's great! You thinking about starting your own business?"

"Kind of."

Linnea's brows pulled together. "What then?"

"I was thinking more of a partnership."

"What do you have in mind? Going into business with Jacob?"

He shook his head as he turned toward her.

"Then wh...?" Her eyes widened.

Here went nothing. He grasped both her hands. "Linnea, I love you." It had gotten easier each time he said it. "Will you be my partner in every area of life? Will you marry me?"

"Logan!" she shrieked as she flung herself into his arms, somehow jumping up and down at the same time. "Yes, yes, *yes!*"

Emotion flooded over him, feelings he'd never expected to own. He clutched her tight against his chest. *Lord, I promise to do everything in my power so she will never regret this moment.*

"I have something for you." He reached into his pocket and pulled out the small wooden box he'd carved. "I hope you like it."

She stroked the satiny finish with one fingertip. "It's beautiful, Logan. I've never seen anything like it."

A thrill ran through him at the recognition. "You haven't even seen inside yet." He tipped the lid open.

Linnea gasped. She reached to touch the ring but pulled back. "For me? Really?"

Logan pulled it out of its navy velvet nest and reached for her left hand. "For you. With all my love, now and for always." He slid the ring onto her finger. A close enough fit for now.

"Logan. The butterflies. I don't know what to say."

The central diamond lay nestled between two tiny butterflies, each with a dainty sapphire on its wings. "When I saw this one, I knew it was perfect."

Her shining eyes lifted to his then her lips invited a kiss. "I love you, Logan Dermott. I can't believe how gorgeous this is."

"I've been thinking..." he murmured against her lips. "Would you like to get married in July? We could go see the Major League Baseball All-Star Game on our honeymoon if you wanted."

"That would be fun." Her face flushed. "If we can tear ourselves out of the hotel room for that long."

"We'll have the rest of our lives, sweetheart." He winked. "I think we can manage a few hours, at least if it isn't the day after the wedding."

"Can we get married in the rose garden at Manito Park? They rent it out sometimes for events."

"That would be perfect. Maybe some butterflies will show up to celebrate with us." A sudden thought struck him. "Maybe we could do a butterfly release afterward. What do you think?"

"I think you thought of everything." Linnea took his face between her hands and kissed him.

Her lips melded against his, and her body curved to fit. Why had he said July? That was too far away. Why not Christmas?

"Are you serious about going away to college next fall?" she asked when they'd come up for air.

He nodded. "I think you and I will be a complementary team in business as well as in life. Between us, we can handle any aspect of customizing people's yards and gardens. Look around you, sweetheart. If we managed this as rookies, think what we can do with training."

Logan loosened his grip on her as she stepped back and turned to view their masterpiece.

"Um, Logan?" she whispered.

"Hmm?"

"We're being watched."

He turned to follow her gaze across the garden and through the wire-mesh fence. Marietta stood on her patio, staring their direction.

Logan bent Linnea over backwards and gave her a big kiss. "That'll tell the busybody everything she needs to know," he murmured as he set Linnea upright.

"The news will be all over Bridgeview by dusk."

He started to chuckle. "Then I guess we'd better get busy finding our friends before she does."

Dear Reader

Do you share my passion for locally grown real food? No, I'm not as fanatical or fixated as many of the characters I write about, but gardening, cooking, and food processing comprise a large part of my non-writing life.

Whether you're new to the concept or a long-time advocate, I invite you to my website and blog at www.valeriecomer.com to explore God's thoughts on the junction of food and faith.

Please sign up for my monthly newsletter while you're there! My gift to all subscribers is *Peppermint Kisses*, a short story set in the Farm Fresh Romance series. Joining my list is the best way to keep tabs on my food/farm life as well as contests, cover reveals, deals, and news about upcoming books. I welcome you!

Enjoy this Book?

Please leave a review at any online retailer or reader site. Letting other readers know what you think about *Secrets of Sunbeams: An Urban Farm Fresh Romance* helps them make a decision and means a lot to me. Thank you!

If you haven't read the original series, the six-book Farm Fresh Romances set on Green Acres Farm, I hope you will. The first story is *Raspberries and Vinegar*.

Keep reading for the first chapter of *Butterflies on Breezes*, the second book in the Urban Farm Fresh Romances.

Memories

of Mist

THE THIRD URBAN FARM FRESH ROMANCE

Chapter One

NO WAY. "A NEW TEACHER?" Adriana Diaz stared at her friend. "What happened to Mrs. Lopez?" She'd been looking forward to this meeting with her daughter's second grade teacher, a woman she'd come to respect in the past three years.

"Her husband got a surprise promotion and transfer to Boston. She notified the school two weeks ago."

Adriana sighed. How had the grapevine missed her? "So what did we get with such short notice?"

Heather Sund grinned. "A hunk." She elbowed Adriana. "Too bad I'm married."

Adriana sighed. The sting of losing Stephan had lessened over the years. That didn't mean she was on a manhunt the way Heather assumed. Raising two kids alone took all the time, energy, and finances she could pull together.

"Violet is going to be crushed." Just like her mother. "Mrs. Lopez is one of the few people who *got* her."

Heather laughed. "Desiree was looking forward to second grade with Mrs. Lopez, too, but she met Mr. Sheridan half an hour ago and she's already decided she's going to marry him someday."

Desiree wasn't Violet. Violet was a challenge, to put it lightly. Adriana dreaded her daughter's teenage years with

241

foreboding as strong as she'd felt the night four years earlier when Stephan had been called out to that fire. Somehow she'd known he wasn't coming home long before the fire chief showed up at her door, hat in hand.

The monitor of Bridgeview Elementary came into the hallway. "Ms. Diaz?"

Heather gave her a nudge. "Is Violet at the playground with Desiree?"

Adriana blinked. "Yes. Would you mind sending her in?"

"My pleasure." She leaned closer and waggled her brows. "Call me later. I want to know what you think of our new teacher."

Um, yeah. Like Adriana was going to walk through the door into the second grade classroom and fall in love with her daughter's new teacher in fifteen minutes flat. "Thanks for getting Violet." She turned and entered the space.

A tall man with dark hair and a short beard stood to meet her, a smile on his face. "Ms. Diaz? And... Violet." He looked behind Adriana. "I'm Mr. Sheridan."

"Yes, I'm Adriana Diaz. My daughter will be here in a minute." She reached out her hand. "It's nice to meet you, Mr. Sheridan."

Heather was right about the hunk part. The man was awfully good looking, and the smile on his face seemed as genuine as his casual shirt and black jeans, just within the dress code for Bridgeview's teachers. To say nothing of how warm his hand felt in hers.

The hand she was still holding. Adriana pulled back. She didn't have time to waste before her daughter entered. There was no way to know whether Violet would bounce in happily, or skulk in with a snarl.

"So you'll be the second grade teacher this year." *Nice*

opening line, Adriana. Smooth.

He shuffled his papers. "Yes, this classroom will house both first and second, since there are so few students in this group. That part hasn't changed."

"It's unusual to find a male teacher in the younger grades. Why did you choose to pursue this age group?"

He blinked, obviously not expecting to defend his choice. "I enjoy children. In the past few years I've taught mostly upper elementary, it's true, but I like the innocence of younger ones. They're not as jaded and bored with the whole school thing yet."

Adriana glanced over her shoulder. "You haven't met Violet. No one has called her innocent since she was a baby."

Mr. Sheridan's smile held. "Each child is an individual. What is your daughter passionate about?"

Picking legs off of flies did not seem to be the appropriate response. "She loves art. And recess."

The man chuckled. "Don't we all love recess? Tell me about your family, Ms. Diaz."

"My husband was a firefighter who died in the line of duty several years ago."

"I'm so sorry to hear that."

"I have two children. My son, Sam, is in third grade, and you'll soon meet Violet. I work from home with two quite different jobs, that of a seamstress and a bookkeeper for several small businesses in Bridgeview." She paused. "How about you, Mr. Sheridan? What are you passionate about?"

"I... uh, teaching."

"What subjects? What are your after-school hobbies?"

"I enjoy cycling and swimming. Skiing when I get a chance. Also, I'm an avid reader. And you, Ms. Diaz?"

The man kept volleying the questions back to her. She

supposed it was fair. After all, she wanted him to understand Violet, and Violet was the sum of her experiences thus far, and that included her home life.

Adriana resisted a shudder. She needed to get some better experiences into her daughter, if that was the case. "I love to cook. You'll find Bridgeview residents share an interest in local food. We have several ongoing initiatives, such as a new community garden that will be ready for next spring. We're also in the process of creating a food forest and, as you know, the Parent Teacher Association has just raised the funds for a greenhouse and fenced garden for the school. How do you plan to take advantage of that space in your teaching?"

He opened and closed his mouth.

She finally had Mr. Sheridan at a loss for words.

"Gardening isn't really my strong suit, and first and second graders don't require it, thankfully. Ms. Bertoli will ably pick up the children's education in this area in third grade."

"Pardon me?" Adriana took a step closer. "You can't be serious. Mrs. Lopez had the entire school year planned around the greenhouse and school garden. The children are looking forward to it, and so are the parents." She narrowed her gaze. "I'm sure the school board made the expectations clear during your interview process, short as it might have been."

"Gardening is not a core curriculum, Ms. Di—"

"It's core in Bridgeview."

"The state—"

"We expect our children to learn reading, writing, and arithmetic, of course. But much as those are useful, there is more to life. Much more, and a healthy approach to food is vital for everyone. That is the reason the PTA worked so hard to make this happen."

"I don't disagree, Ms. Diaz, but the teaching approach may vary." The teacher's smile looked forced. "I have a full year planned without a gardening component. I'm sure you'll understand."

"No, I don't. The greenhouse is there for every classroom, and the parents of Bridgeview Elementary School expect it to be used."

Bet he could hardly wait until her fifteen minutes was up and he could meet the next parents. But this wasn't something Adriana was willing to concede. Not after all the fundraising and grant-writing and everything the PTA had gone through. Her daughter needed this type of curriculum now, this year.

"Hi, Mom. Is this my new teacher? What happened to Mrs. Lopez?"

Adriana turned. Her child stood in the doorway, feet planted and arms crossed as she stared over at the man.

"Mr. Sheridan, my daughter, Violet. Violet, this is Mr. Sheridan."

"How come he's a man? Where's Mrs. Lopez?"

She'd skip the first question. "Mrs. Lopez moved to Boston, so she can't be your teacher after all."

"Hi, Violet. I'm pleased to meet you. We're going to have a really good school year. Your mom says you like art—"

"I want gardening class. My mom told me there'd be outside stuff in the greenhouse."

"Next year, when you're in third grade."

Violet's chin came out and her voice rose. "That's not fair. That's Sam's grade. I want it now. Mom said."

Myles Sheridan stared at the belligerent girl with her arms crossed in front of her. The only thought he could summon was thankfulness the child was in second grade, not first, and he'd only have to deal with her one year. *Forgive me, Lord. I know every child is important, and this one is no exception.*

But gardening? The board had mentioned the greenhouse acquisition, of course, but not a single member had balked when he stated that his class wouldn't be making use of it. No one had warned him about Ms. Diaz or her daughter.

The expression on both faces was similar. Not particularly friendly. The mother had seemed pleasant — cordial, even — when she first entered, but now her lips were drawn into a tight line and her brown eyes flashed dangerously, not diminishing her natural beauty.

He'd met a mom or two with an agenda in his previous schools. Myles generated a smile for the child. Once she was won over, her mother would back off. "What was your favorite thing about this summer, Violet?"

She shoved her long blond hair off her face. "I went to the rodeo with my grandma and grandpa. There were even kids doing mutton bustin'. That looked like fun, but my grandpa said I couldn't try."

"Mutton busting?" That was a new one. Myles couldn't help glancing at Ms. Diaz.

"Sheep riding, like bull riding for kids. The kid who stays aboard the longest wins."

"I see." He looked back at Violet. "I hope you'll draw me a picture of that event on the first day of school."

The child shrugged. "Maybe."

246

Myles glanced at the clock on the wall. The next parent and child were likely waiting in the hallway by now. "It's been nice meeting you, Violet. Ms. Diaz. School starts at 8:30 on Tuesday. I look forward to making this your best school year ever." That line seemed to have more of a ring to it when he taught sixth grade.

"Before we go, Mr. Sheridan, I'd like to hear you address some ideas for use of the greenhouse space for your class. This is something the PTA has worked hard to bring to Bridgeview Elementary, and we're not about to let one rogue teacher derail our program."

"I hardly think I'm de—"

"How would you feel if your child's second grade teacher didn't think reading was important, Mr. Sheridan? Is it okay to take a year or two off? The children can always pick it up later, right?"

"Excuse me, Ms. Diaz. I hardly think this falls in the same category. You are talking about a garden."

"There are adults who do not read, Mr. Sheridan. Some who cannot, and some who can't be bothered. I'm a reader myself, and I read to Violet and her brother every day. But it is possible to function in society with very limited reading ability."

He crossed his arms and leaned against his desk. "Your point?"

"My point is that everyone in America eats every day, whether or not they read. Yes, some are more fortunate than others as to the choices they are offered, but an early introduction to the basics of nutrition is vital in this day of childhood obesity, to say nothing of society's obsession with technology. Learning to grow food hands-on will open as many doors to our children as reading."

She couldn't be serious. School gardening class as an antidote to childhood obesity? As important as reading? He met her unyielding gaze. She was absolutely serious.

"I'll consider it." That was the best he could offer to clear the air and make way for meeting the next family.

"I look forward to hearing you plans for implementation soon. I'll be speaking to the school board about this, though. They were negligent if they didn't make sure a new hire understood the situation."

Myles scratched his neck. He hadn't been hauled into the principal's office since he was a kid. Hadn't this been what it felt like? "I did say I'll contemplate it."

"Great choice. I'm not letting this go, Mr. Sheridan." She turned to her daughter. "Coming, Violet?"

The child smirked at him as she went through the doorway, her mother's hand on her shoulder.

Myles let out a long breath. Fit a greenhouse into his carefully written plans... or face this obstinate mother-daughter pair. They were going to be the death of him.

Memories of Mist

is available where you purchased

Secrets of Sunbeams

and

Butterflies on Breezes

Author Biography

Valerie Comer lives where food meets faith in her real life, her fiction, and on her blog and website. She and her husband of over 35 years farm, garden, and keep bees on a small farm in Western Canada, where they grow and preserve much of their own food.

Valerie has always been interested in real food from scratch, but her conviction has increased dramatically since God blessed her with three delightful granddaughters. In this world of rampant disease and pollution, she is compelled to do what she can to make these little girls' lives the best she can. She helps supply healthy food — local food, organic food, seasonal food — to grow strong bodies and minds.

Valerie is a *USA Today* bestselling author and a two-time Word Award winner. She has been called "a stellar storyteller" as she injects experience laced with humor into her green clean romances.

To find out more, visit her website at www.valeriecomer.com, where you can read her blog, explore her many links, and sign up for her email newsletter to download the free short story: *Peppermint Kisses: A (short) Farm Fresh Romance 2.5*. You can also use this QR code to access the newsletter sign-up.